A DANCE WITH LOVE AND MURDER

BOOK 1

TERRY L. PASS

Book Cover by Rockingbookcovers.com

Edited by Banks L.

"For we are not out mistakes, but the lessons we learn from them."

– T. L. Pass

CONTENTS

DEDICATION

FIRST AND FOREMOST, GIVING glory and honor to God, who not only is the reason why I'm here, but blessed me with the talent to hear and tell stories. If it were not for God I would be lost and never understand the true meaning of love and my purpose in life.

Secondly, this book and all my works are dedicated to my parents, Jerome and Anita Pass, and Velma Davis. There aren't enough words to accurately describe what you all mean to me. Raising me and providing for me is the simplest thing you all ever did. All three of you have blessed me with wisdom, discernment, the full capability to love, and the knowledge of how to carry myself in this world. All that I am, and all I will be is because of the lessons you all gave me. My only regret in life is that I can't give this copy to all three of you. I love you all and I hope I made you proud.

Thirdly, my siblings, Teidru, Tarnesha, Eddie, Terrance and Brandon. This is also dedicated to you all because I would be nothing without you. As your little brother, I have watched all of you succeed and struggle. But through it all we had each other. I love you all, and please celebrate in that this is only the beginning!!

PROLOGUE

On the Southside of Chicago in the early 1990s, the only thing more common than violence was the Red Line screeching to a halt. When the sun warmed the humid air, territory made even a timid child a fierce warrior just to make it through the end of the day. On East 75th Street, two blocks from the 75th and Grand Crossing Red Line station, was a haven for the Southside. There was only one house on the block that sat between two churches and a police station across the street. Most of the Sunday crowd and patrolmen paid little attention to the brick two-story house. With its half-kept yard and rusting green metal chairs on the porch, the house was more of a neighborhood monument than a residence. The only semblance of habitation was a little kid named Denzel dribbling his basketball in front of the house.

Denzel spent the first ten years of his life on the south side of Chicago. Like every child on the south side, his heroes were the sports stars who called the windy city home. Denzel covered almost every inch of his room with Bulls, Bears, or White Sox posters. But there was one poster that hung prominently at the head of his bed, and that was of Michael Jordan. Jordan was the most famous black person on the planet during the late eighties and early nineties. But to every little black kid in America, he was like the second coming of Christ. To Denzel, his love of Jordan was only second to his mother. To him, she was the perfect parent. She was a best friend, disciplinarian, scholar, and his only example of love.

Denzel's mother, Verna, assumed both parental roles in their household after the murder of his father, Jerome when Denzel was a toddler. The pain of watching the love of her life being murdered was too heavy for Verna to spread to Denzel. Lying to him seemed like the best option, but the older Denzel got, the harder it was to tell him the truth. Extinguishing his glow didn't seem as important as protecting him. So, to keep his light and her secret buried, Verna told Denzel his father left after he was born. Whenever Denzel would ask about him, she told him they met in the Army, and he left them before deployment, then died in combat. Verna poured in all that a man should be, hoping to make Denzel better than his father. Unfortunately, Denzel never got that full lesson because his mother left before she could give it.

Verna's death began on an early June morning. The air had warmed a little, so Denzel could still feel the coolness of his bedroom window on his fingertips. Normally, an early school-less morning would fill Denzel up with excitement, but today was the last day before his mother deployed again. He lay in his bed with his eyes closed, mapping out their last day together. The day before Verna deployed, she and Denzel followed the same routine as they had done since Denzel could remember. They would start with breakfast at IHOP, then maybe a movie or shopping in the afternoon. In the evening, they would head down to the Navy Pier and watch the sunset, eating ice cream or drinking something warm.

After a while, Denzel couldn't take any more thinking about his last day with his mother, so he got the day started. He got up, brushed his teeth, and reluctantly walked downstairs toward the smell of bacon. As he swung around the end of the banister, he saw his mother's military bags packed and sitting in front of the end table by the front door. On the couch next to the end table was his Grandmother Pearl, sipping coffee and looking at the news on the television.

"Hey, Grandma Pearl," he said, his voice monotone.

"Oh, I know my one and only grandson didn't just greet me like that. Boy, you better get over here and act like you love me."

Denzel decided not to hold back his smile and ran to his grandmother and then jumped on her. Pearl, setting her coffee down just in time, let out a whoop when he landed. Verna popped her head through the pale white swinging door leading to the kitchen and said, "Boy, what did I tell you about running in this house?"

"Leave the boy alone, Verna," Pearl said, giving Denzel a bear hug. "The boy ain't seen his grandmother in a year. I thought you had a grown man living with you for a second." She laughed.

Verna laughed as she saw Denzel wiggling to get free. "Momma, he eats like one, so you may not be able to do that soon. But no matter how old he is, he'll get a whooping if he runs through this house again."

Denzel turned his head with a smile, writhing in pain. Verna let a smile break and said, "Let that boy go so he can eat his breakfast."

"My breakfast?" Denzel asked, appalled through gasped air. Denzel assumed that the smell of bacon was his grandma's breakfast. "We always go to IHOP before you leave," He whined as he pushed open the swinging door. When he walked into the kitchen, he gazed at a table full of waffles, eggs, bacon, sausage, home fries, fruit, and two fresh juices.

"Well, I made you breakfast because I had to save money." She reached into her robe pocket and pulled out two tickets. "Since we are going to see the Bulls play the Lakers tonight for game one of the finals."

Denzel's mouth would have dropped to the floor if it could. He was not only going to see his first NBA game, but he was also going to see Michael Jordan play. His first thought was of all his classmates being jealous when he told him what he did over the summer.

"Thank you so much Mommy." He hugged her as tight as he could, trying not to cry from his excitement. Verna kissed

Denzel on the head, trying to hold back her own tears, scared she would never see him again after today.

"Alright, hurry and finish your breakfast. We still have a lot to do before then." She said, turning away before a tear could fall. Pearl walked into the kitchen, complaining about her being left out of the invitation for breakfast. "Momma, you never needed an invitation for anything in your life." Verna laughed.

After breakfast, Verna and Denzel headed to the aquarium, then a quick stop at the planetarium. While Verna had fun showing Denzel every placard of facts she could, Denzel's attention never left the game waiting for tipoff. He jumped through every doorway with his tongue out or pretending to give Verna no-look passes with nonexistent basketballs. Eventually, it was time to head to the Chicago Stadium. The whole train ride, Denzel asked every question that came to his mind about an NBA game. Where were the seats? How loud would it get? Could he pee in an empty cup so he didn't miss anything? It got to be so much that Verna told him if he didn't be quiet, they were going back home. When they finally got to their seats, however, Denzel was speechless. Although they were not anywhere near the court, Denzel couldn't tell any different.

"Are you happy?" Verna finally asked after about 15 minutes of silence. "I know I couldn't get us the best seats, but these were the best I could get."

"This is perfect, momma. Look! " Denzel said, almost falling in the row in front of him. "Michael is right there. I mean, he's right there! Michael!" He yelled waving his hand frantically over his head. Denzel knew Jordan was probably more focused on playing in his first finals game than the kid was calling his name. But, if he could get him to look towards his section, it would be the perfect highlight for him.

Denzel became mesmerized by the time the game started. He tried not to even so much as blink so he wouldn't miss anything. When the Bulls scored, the crowd erupted into cheer. Then Jordan double-clutched and dunked the ball on a fast break, and the arena went berserk. Even with the Lakers winning the game, Denzel couldn't get over how close the game was. He couldn't wait to get back home to give Grandma Pearl a complete play-by-play.

"Geesh, Verna, you would think the boy played the way he is talking about that game," Pearl said, as Denzel gave her a twenty-minute incoherent spill as soon as he walked through the door.

"Imagine being there with him, Momma." Verna chuckled. She turned to look at Denzel's overjoyed face and said, "Go ahead and put all that energy you have into getting ready for bed." Sensing his mother's impending mood switch, he hugged and kissed Grandma Pearl goodnight. He turned to hug his mother, and the realization of her departure sunk in his heart. A tear tracked down his face and stained his mother's shirt.

"Aw boo-bear, I'm going to miss you too," Verna said, feeling his sadness in her heart. "Now go upstairs, and I'll come to tuck you in before I leave." Verna always left for her assignments at night, figuring it would be easier on him and her, but it was never easy.

After Denzel's shower, he brushed his teeth and got into bed, awaiting the sound of his mother's climb up the stairs. When she finally came up, Denzel had already been asleep for about an hour.

"Denzel, I'm about to leave," Verna said, sneaking into his room.

"Mommy, I don't want you to go," He said, wiping his eyes. "Can't you find a new job?"

"I'm so sorry, baby, but it doesn't work like that," she said as she sat on the side of his bed. "There are bad people in the world, and I have to protect my battle buddies and, most importantly, you."

"You mean how I protect you, right?"

"Yes, you do, baby. You're my little hero. Now, I need you to be Grandma Pearl's hero, too. She is getting old, but don't you tell her I said that!" She laughed.

Verna gave Denzel one last hug and kiss, and she crept out of his room. Her silhouette escaped the touch of his night light, and he watched her disappear into the darkness.

When Denzel woke the following morning to the smell of bacon sizzling in the pan again, he thought maybe his mom didn't leave. He rushed downstairs and burst through the swinging door, only to see his grandmother cooking breakfast and his ninja turtle suitcase by the kitchen door.

"Boy, stop running through here scaring me like that," Pearl said, stopping herself from hurling a pair of tongs at his head. "Now hurry up and get in the shower. We are going to hit the road when you finish eating!" She said, turning back to the stove and balancing the tongs on the edge of the skillet and counter.

"Where are we going?" Denzel asked, kneeling down to open his suitcase. He opened it and watched what seemed like all the clothes in his dresser erupting onto the floor. "Am I moving?" He asked, peaking his head back in the kitchen.

"Oh, baby, I ain't risking our lives here." She said, putting his plate on the kitchen table. "I have been trying to get your momma to move for years. Children don't need to grow up around stray bullets. And you're old enough to travel now, so we are driving to Virginia. Now," she said, seeing his mouth gaped open. "Your momma knows where to send all your little letters. And we'll be there before she gets to where she will be. Now, go wash up and eat. We have a long drive ahead of us."

Disappointed at spending his summer out in the country, he knew better than to talk back. Denzel did what he was told without uttering a single word of agitation. After a while, Pearl packed her Ford Explorer, gassed up, and pulled onto I-90, which was heading towards Norfolk, Virginia. The drive to the south seemed like the most excruciating experience of Denzel's life. He had never been to his grandmother's house before, so when he couldn't sleep anymore, he imagined how Norfolk looked. He imagined a big farm where he would have to work from sunup to sundown. Or some place in the woods where there wouldn't be another kid his age for miles around.

As they drove into the Hampton Roads area of Virginia, Pearl pointed out landmarks after hearing how disappointed Denzel was to live in the country. "Denzel, baby, there is the Hampton Coliseum. If you only knew the nights, I couldn't remember going to concerts there." Pearl laughed. She changed the subject when she saw the question forming on his face. "When we get to the tunnel, I want you to see if you can hold your breath until we get to the other side."

"What tunnel?" Denzel asked. As the words escaped his mouth, he looked out onto the water on both sides of the bridge. "We're going underwater?"

"Well, we're definitely not going through a mountain." Grandma Pearl chuckled. Denzel was so fascinated about a tunnel that went underwater, that he forgot to hold his breath. Before long the idea of farm lands were also far from his mind when Denzel saw the shopping centers, buildings and traffic.

When they finally arrived in Pearl's neighborhood, Denzel couldn't believe that it reminded him of his neighborhood. The street, lined with houses, had children playing in front of them. Denzel was becoming impatient to get out of the car and finally play with kids his age. When Pearl pulled in front of her house,

Denzel darted out of the car toward the kid playing basketball in his driveway next door.

"Boy, if you don't bring in this suitcase! What, you think I'm your servant?" Pearl yelled. "Devon is not moving anytime soon, so he'll be here when you get done putting your things away."

A couple of weeks later, the worst day of Denzel's life found him. He got up early that morning, still thinking about playing "hide and go get" with Devon and some neighborhood kids the night prior. Everyone there could tell that Denzel had never played before with the confusion on his face when they gathered in a circle.

Then, finally, Devon took him over by the tree in front of Grandma Peal's house and said, "Man, I'm trying to get you some girls, but you are coming off weird, dude. Look, you see them over there. They are already scrunching their face and pointing, and we haven't started yet."

Denzel looked at where Devon was pointing, and sure enough, it was just as he said. He turned back to Devon and said, "I don't even know what hide and go get is."

Devon shook his head trying not to laugh. "It's just like hide and go seek, but if you're 'it,' you have to find a girl to kiss. Now stop acting weird. You're the new guy, and girls love the new guy. Look, you see that tall, light-skinned girl? That's Nicole. She lives across the street from the corner store. One day, she's going to be my girl, and word is her sister Keisha likes you."

"Well, which one is Keisha?"

Devon grabbed Denzel by the top of the head and directed it into Keisha's awaiting eyes. Keisha was short, had dark skin, and was the prettiest girl on the street. Sweat forming in Denzel's hands, he turned back to Devon and said, "Look, man, I don't know about this. How about I see how it's played once, then I'll play."

Devon punched him on the shoulder. "Look, do you like girls or not?" Denzel nodded with a painful grimace on his face. "Ok then, let's play and stop acting like you're scared. Now, follow my lead."

Devon and Denzel walked back over to the group, pretending like they weren't holding the game up. Denzel lined up with the others as Devon proceeded to the center. Then Devon clapped his hands loudly and said, "Ok, I'm it."

All the girls rolled their eyes and mumbled, "He always wants to be it."

Devon covered his eyes and started counting down from twenty. And before Denzel knew it, Keisha grabbed his hand and scattered like everyone else. She led him under the tree in Pearl's backyard. Its leaves flowed down to the grass blades, covering anything standing behind it.

"So, what do we do now?" Denzel asked so nervously, that he could barely finish his sentence.

"Well, you can wait and see if Devon finds me first, or you can beat him to it and kiss me now." She said, pulling Denzel closer to her. And under that tree, hidden in the darkness, he had his first kiss. They completely forgot about the game and kissed until they heard Pearl's voice yelling for Denzel to come inside. Before he left, Denzel asked Keisha to be his girlfriend. She looked him in the eyes and said, "I already am."

Denzel replayed every second of the night over in his head as he poured a big bowl of cereal the next morning. But as soon as he sat down to eat, he heard a knock at the door.

When he opened the door, he expected to see Keisha, but it was a very tall white man in a military uniform. He wore a dark green suit with a lot of medals on his chest and yellow stripes and symbols on his sleeve. In his hand, there was an American flag folded in a triangle.

"Hey, little guy, is your grandmother home?" He asked, kneeling down.

"Who wants to know?" Denzel asked his guard up.

"Can you go get her, please? I have to give her an urgent message. I'll wait out here." He said, standing back up and stepping back a few feet from the door.

Denzel shut and locked the door, then ran upstairs. When he got to his grandmother's room, he yelled, "Grandma, Grandma! Wake up. Some man in a uniform wants you at the door!"

Grandma Pearl awoke in a frantic, preparing to attack when she saw Denzel's scared face. "Denzel! I'm not going to tell you again. Stop yelling like that to wake me up. Why are you always so loud? What, you think the louder you are, the faster I'm going to get up?" She sat on the edge of the bed to catch her breath, then said, "Now, what do you want?"

Embarrassed at upsetting her, Denzel hung his head low and said, "There is a man in a uniform asking for you at the door."

"Pick your head up, Denzel, ain't nobody yelling at you. I swear you're sensitive like your mother." She put her slippers on and walked down the stairs to answer the door. Denzel crept behind her as she made her way downstairs. First, she looked through the peephole, assessing her visitor. Then Grandma Pearl got stiff. She held the same position for a few seconds before turning around and shooing Denzel back upstairs.

"Why? I don't want to leave you by yourself." Denzel told her.

Then she snapped, "Dammit, Denzel Eugene Williams, do as I tell you!"

Denzel ran upstairs and disappeared from her view. He peeked around the corner at the top of the stairs, wiping tears from her eyes. Pearl opened the door and started talking to the man in a soft tone. Still determined, Denzel crept down the stairs and saw Pearl break out in a hysterical cry and hugged the man. As she let go, he handed her the folded flag, and she squeezed it against her chest and closed the door, thanking the man. At that point, Denzel didn't care if she has caught him sneaking. He knew in his stomach that his mother wasn't coming home.

Pearl turned around and saw him sitting on the stairs, but her face couldn't hide her pain. She tried, but it was the type of pain that you can't fake. A kind of pain that is life-changing and takes a lifetime to dissipate.

CHAPTER I

A NIGHT OUT

WHOOP! WHOOP! WHOOP!

The blaring alarm jolted me awake. The darkness of the room sent a wave of panic through me. "Did I sleep through the night? What time is it?" I muttered, scrambling to find my phone beneath the pillows. As I silenced the alarm, the screen lit up—9:30 PM, Saturday, June 13. The remembrance that today was the anniversary of my mother's passing instantly reactivated my emotional defenses. Before I could dismiss the reminder and bury the date, my phone buzzed with a text from Devon:

I'm on my way!

I set the phone down and rolled back over. After a grueling 16-hour shift at the hospital and a mere three hours of sleep, my body screamed for rest. But even more than sleep, I dreaded being alone. My phone vibrated again.

Negro, you better be out of bed. I know you.

I rolled my eyes in annoyance and tossed the phone aside. It wasn't even my idea to go out, yet there was Devon, hurrying me as if I were delaying him.

Now fully awake, I stretched an arm across the other side of the bed, longing for her presence. How far had I fallen? I sat up, running my hands through the remnants of waves in my hair. I could easily find a reason to cancel, but I owed Devon this. Besides, what was the worst that could happen? Reaching for my phone, I was about to confirm our plans when Devon preempted me with another message, reminding me we were headed to The Granby Theatre and to dress nicely. The Granby Theatre, a recently revamped nightclub in Norfolk, drew crowds from all six surrounding cities of Hampton Roads, Virginia. It seemed like just the place to shake off my gloom.

I got up, walked around the bed, and headed into the bathroom to get ready. Turning on the shower, I closed the door to let the steam accumulate. Soon, steam seeped from beneath the shower curtain, fogging the mirror. I watched my reflection blur as I recalled the last time I saw Gianna.

It was six months ago. I sat alone, hands damp with sweat, nervously fidgeting with a ring box. It was the most nervous I had ever felt. I wasn't perfect, but I believed I could be perfect for her. A seven o'clock reservation awaited us at a French restaurant with views of the oceanfront. Gianna was usually on time, but that evening, she was uncharacteristically late. It wasn't until 7:45 that I spotted her approaching the maître d' to inquire about our table. When she rounded the host stand, my heart thumped violently. She looked breathtaking. Gianna, with her mixed heritage, carried the striking features of both her black and white ancestries. She was wearing her favorite blush-colored sheath dress that hugged her curves just right and fell to her knees. Her long, dark brown hair cascaded down her back. She was perfection.

As she locked eyes with me and approached the table, I panicked, shoving the ring into my pocket before standing to greet her. Unbeknownst to me, the warmth was not mutual. As I moved to hug her, she scoffed, pulled out her chair, and sat down. Oblivious to her cold demeanor, I assumed it was as good a time as any to propose.

I pulled the ring box from my pocket and dropped to one knee. As I reached for her hand to begin my speech, the surrounding clatter grew, and I felt the gaze of onlookers upon us. Phones emerged from pockets, and cameras flashed. Then Gianna burst into hysterical laughter. Leaning back, she shouted, "Are you fucking serious? You think I'm going to marry a piece of shit like you?" Her laughter intensified as confusion spread across my face, prompting her to continue. "I gave you multiple chances, and you still screwed it up. It's bad enough that you got her pregnant, but then you..." Her voice trailed off as she noticed the camera phones pointed at us. Scooting back her chair abruptly, she declared, "You know what? I'm done with this conversation, and I'm done with you. I swear, Denzel, you will get what's coming to you. Believe that."

She turned and stormed out. There I was, still on one knee, the snickers of spectators mingling with the blinding flashes of their cameras. I scrambled to my feet and chased after her, bursting out of the restaurant only to see her walking toward a car just beyond the valet stand.

"Gianna, wait!" I yelled, sprinting toward her.

She glanced back as she opened the passenger side door and said, "Before you give me some bullshit excuse about how sorry you are, think about Tara and what you did to her." Climbing into the car, she left me standing there, dumbfounded. The car peeled away, and with it, Gianna exited my life forever.

Memories of what I'd done to Tara and Gianna replayed in my mind on a constant loop. I used to think it drove me insane, but now I see it as a blessing. How can I become a better man unless I acknowledge and change my flaws? I opened the bathroom door, releasing the trapped steam, and heard my phone ringing on the bed. "Damn, that's Devon, and he's probably outside already." Just as I suspected, it was Devon calling.

"Yeah?" I groaned.

"Come outside!" Devon yelled through the phone, his music blaring in the background. I don't know why he never turns the volume down when talking on the phone.

"Can you turn the music down so my neighbors don't—"

"What?!" he interrupted. "Hold on. Let me turn down the music for your whispering ass."

I didn't reply; I knew that conversation was a dead end. I've known Devon too long. "Look, I just need to put my clothes on. I'll be out in a minute." I wanted to look sharp but feel comfortable, so I chose a simple V-neck shirt and nice slacks, snug enough to show off my muscles.

"You better be looking like a sex magnet," he said.

"Shut the hell up, Devon," I snapped back.

"Oh, it ain't 'V' no more? Nah, we're putting everyone's government names out now."

"Are you ever going to speak proper English? You forget you have a master's degree."

"Yeah, but I got my Ph.D. from the block. And since you've got so many problems with how I talk, come outside and give me a lesson then, bitch!"

I hung up. Devon always knew how to push my buttons, making me want to knock him out. He knows I'll react, forcing me to confront him faster. He's the only person who can get under my skin like that. More than a best friend or a brother, Devon is like a twin separated at birth.

I walked out of my apartment to the parking lot and saw Devon leaning against his convertible Camaro.

"Z, what up, my dude!? Took you long enough. I swear a woman gets ready faster," he laughed.

"Kiss my ass, and I'm driving. That way, I don't have to wait for you when I'm ready to leave," I said, heading to my BMW coupe. He reluctantly climbed in, and we drove off toward downtown Norfolk.

"Why did you pick tonight to go out? Didn't you start your morning shifts this weekend?" I asked.

"Yeah," he said with a grin, "but I've got some dirt on my supervisor, Mr. Roberts, so I'm not starting those shifts until next weekend. I have to go in on Monday for training, but I ain't showing up until like 10."

"What do you have on him?" I asked, eyeing his smirk.

"You're not going to believe me if I tell you."

"Try me."

"Boom," he started, clapping his hand with a punch. "So, about two weeks ago, I was working my usual night shift, handling updates and other stuff. Around midnight, I went to drop off some reports and walked in on Mr. Roberts getting some neck action from this badass woman."

"Wait, run that back," I interrupted.

"I told you wouldn't believe me."

"Are you trying to tell me your supervisor, Dana Roberts—Mr. 'my belly sticks out further than my dick' Roberts—had some woman in his office giving him head?"

"My dude," Devon leaned against the passenger door, "she wasn't just some woman. I only saw her from the back, but she was fine. Plus, this dumbass was holding onto the American Flag when I walked in and almost knocked it over." We both erupted with laughter. "Needless to say, when Mr. Roberts saw me, he knew I had him."

Wiping tears from my eyes, I said, "Thanks, man. I needed that laugh."

"That's why I wanted you to come out tonight. I haven't really seen you since you and Gianna split. I mean, I had to send an email invite at work just to get your attention. But I knew you needed something to take your mind off things."

"I can't lie; I'm not doing great. Gianna is constantly on my mind, and I can't shut it off."

"Bro, what happened? It seemed like everything was good, especially when you bought the ring. You guys were supposed to be the poster couple for a perfect biracial relationship."

I chuckled. "Yeah, you'd think."

"She found out about another hoe, didn't she?" His tone was more accusatory than comedic.

I paused, thinking of Tara and what I had done to her. "Yeah, she went in for a doctor's visit, and of all the doctors, it was Gianna who treated her. I guess she saw my face on the lock screen of Gianna's phone." Afraid he would see through my lies, I kept my gaze fixed on the window.

"Well, I don't feel sorry for your dumbass. You had a good thing with Gianna, but you had to go and mess it up, like always."

"No, you're right. I need to change." The memories of my last moments with Tara were brewing in my mind, and I needed to drown them out. So, I cranked up the music to quiet my thoughts and sped towards Granby Street.

Finding parking on Granby Street was always a challenge, so I opted for the mall's parking garage on the next street. I dated the woman who worked at the booth, and she always let me park there for free. So, we parked in my usual spot in the employee section and headed to Granby Street.

Granby Street is a vibrant section of Norfolk where the locals gather to party. There were souped-up cars cruising slowly through the streets, inebriated women shouting randomly, and strands of lights hanging overhead to illuminate the scene. And at the heart of it all was the Granby Theatre. By day, it served as an actual theater for local productions, but on weekends, they cleared out the hall, transforming it into the hottest club in Norfolk.

When we entered the club, the waves of bass were so powerful I could feel them vibrating through my body. Holding a regular conversation was going to be impossible, so we immediately launched into our "divide and conquer" strategy. Devon headed to the dance floor, and I made my way to the bar. This had been our plan since college. The only difference now, since Devon is committed to his childhood sweetheart, Nicole, is that I've been handling the conquering solo for the last few years.

Once I reached the bar, I flagged down the bartender. Then, I felt a voice whisper faintly in my ear, "What are you buying me?"

CHAPTER 2

ONE LAST TIME

I TURNED TO MY right, toward the source of the voice requesting a drink. Standing next to me was a stunning woman in a tight black cocktail dress, her eyes locking onto mine. She was tall, with dreadlocks pulled into a bun, and her beautiful, dark skin seemed to glow. I looked at her from head to toe, admiring her body. Her physique was the kind that showed dedication to the gym. Her face was flawless, and her brown eyes were mesmerizing, drawing me in deeper the longer I looked.

"Excuse me?" I managed trying to maintain my composure.

She leaned in and gave my earlobe a soft pinch. "I said, what are you getting me to drink?"

"Am I being hit on right now?" I chuckled.

"No, I'm asking you for a drink. I'm thirsty," she replied plainly.

With the thumping music drowning out any chance of normal conversation, I conceded to her request. I flagged down the bartender. "Yeah, my man," I yelled over the music, "Can she get a—"

"Melon ball!" she shouted.

I looked at her, pleasantly surprised by her choice. Then back, to the bartender, "And a Jack and Coke for me." I yelled.

"You starting a tab?" the bartender shouted back.

I glanced at the woman as she gave me a cocky grin, and handed my card to the bartender. When I did, she smiled as if it had been her plan all along. I pulled her close to speak into her ear again.

But as she drew near, she started dancing against me. Her body moved slowly, pressing harder against me with each sway. She turned to face me, pulled my head down, and said, "My name is Simone by the way," loudly in my ear.

"Denzel," I said back into her ear. "Do you want to go to the smoking section with me outside?"

"I don't smoke."

"Neither do I, but I would like to us to have a conversation. Plus," I added, pointing to the crowd of intoxicated dancers, "this isn't my scene." She nodded, and we grabbed our drinks and made our way out the back of the club.

Outside, there was a small triangle-shaped gated area for smokers. The gates were tall, with black bars spaced close enough to provide a view but too narrow for anyone to slip through.

"So, Ms. Simone," I began once we reached the empty smoke pit, "out of all the guys in the club, what gives me the honor of buying you a drink?"

"You looked like you could afford it," she said, a playful snicker escaping her lips.

"You are hilarious. I like that in a woman," I said, laughing along.

"You assume this drink is going to lead you somewhere."

"Is it not? I mean, am I not worth it?" I asked, leaning my back against the bars and smiling at her.

"Well, I don't know you well enough to judge your worth, but I admit, you're cute," she said, taking a sip through her black cocktail straw.

"Cuteness has to be worth some points, right?"

She chuckled. "Cuteness is to describe babies and puppies. I don't want a cute man."

As she turned to walk back into the club, I reached out and gently grabbed her arm to stop her. Just then, I noticed a young black woman watching us, cigarette in hand. Conscious of how it might look, I quickly let go. As soon as I released her arm, a group of preppy college students came out for a smoke.

"Hear me out," I pleaded in a low voice as she turned back to me, pausing and glancing at her lit phone screen, clearly indicating I was on a time limit.

"I enjoy talking to you, and I guarantee you'll have more fun with me out here, even with the second-hand smoke, than you will inside."

"And how can you be so sure?" she smirked.

"Because I don't think you've accomplished what you set out to do."

"What makes you think that? I mean, I asked you for a drink and," she took another sip, "I have that. So, it seems like you won't meet your goals for the night."

"And what makes you think I have a goal?" I asked, finishing the last of my drink.

"Every man that comes to a club has a goal. Guys don't come here to dance. It's all foreplay to you guys."

"Ah, you see, normally you would be right," I countered as I paced to position myself with my back to the college kids who were smoking. "The only variable you haven't considered is that I could be the anomaly."

"Every guy says he's an anomaly before he tries to get with the woman he's pursuing."

"And this is where you're wrong. I'm not trying to get with you," I clarified.

Simone rolled her eyes and retorted, "That's bullshit."

"I'm serious. I've been down this road many times and know what demons are there."

"Demons?" Her tone shifted from skeptical to intrigued.

"There's always a demon trying to rip away at my happiness. It's either snatched away from me, or I mess it up," I explained, gazing at the tops of the surrounding buildings before returning my focus to her warm brown eyes. "When you put your all into those you love, and it always ends in heartbreak, you learn not to try anymore. I enjoy talking with you, Simone, and if something happens between us, it will. But my mindset going into this is just an evening full of conversation and sarcasm, nothing more."

She smirked.

"Oh, my crushed heart amuses you," I joked. "You are evil."

The thick smell of cigarette smoke began to burn my nostrils. I turned to see that the once-empty smoke pit had filled up quickly. Suggesting we leave, I took Simone by the hand, closed my tab, and led her through the club. We exited onto Granby Street, laughing and joking as we walked as if we had known each other for years. She felt both familiar and new. We strolled down to the piers and circled back, eventually making our way to a rooftop bar near the Granby Theatre. As soon as we sat down around the fire pit with our drinks, my phone vibrated in my pocket.

I pulled out my phone and saw a text from Devon:

Negro, I know you didn't leave without me.

I glanced at Simone with my mouth hanging open in shock. She looked at me, her head tilted curiously.

"I completely forgot to tell you, I'm here with my friend Devon and—"

"And let me guess," she interrupted, smiling, "you drove." I nodded. "Well then, I guess you'll have to add one more passenger." Her fingers brushed the back of my hand gently.

"Simone, we don't have to do this."

She stood up, kissed me on the lips, and whispered, "Just because you're not looking to hook up doesn't mean I can't still have my fun." She caressed my jawline smoothly, her touch lingering on my face, and said, "Now, introduce me to your friend."

I stood up without hesitation and walked her back to my car. When Simone and I reached the garage, Devon was leaning against it, smoking a blunt. He complained that my delay was the reason he had to wait so long. I called him a coon as I snatched the blunt from his hand and took a few hits. Smoking wasn't my normal vice, but tonight felt like the night to indulge. I gestured to Devon and introduced him. "Simone, meet my friend."

"You're just as rude as you are ugly," Devon quipped, sizing me up before turning to Simone with a flirtatious grin. "How are you doing, sweetheart? My name's V."

"I'm good," she smiled. "Is he always this rude?" They both shared a laugh at my expense.

"Yeah, yeah, yeah. Y'all can be funny all you want, but don't find yourselves stranded in this parking garage," I said, opening my driver's door. Devon folded down the passenger seat and climbed into the back, while Simone settled into the passenger seat after inspecting the inside of my car.

As we pulled away, Devon, ever the overprotective brother, started his usual interrogation. "So, Simone, what are you?"

Simone turned sharply to look at him in the backseat and said, “What do you mean?”

I chuckled and clarified, “I think he means to ask about your race. Devon here assumes every woman with locs must have ties to the islands.”

“First off,” Devon interjected, “I’m usually right because they often are. And second, how the hell are you going to throw out my government name like its nothing? You don’t know her. She could be the FBI.”

“If I were in the FBI, your name would be the easiest thing to know about you,” Simone retorted.

I laughed, catching Devon’s eye in the rearview mirror. “Ahh, she got you good.”

Simone turned back around, laughing. “You guys seem more like brothers than friends.”

"Man, Z wishes he had my DNA," Devon said. "If he did, he wouldn't be driving this dumb-ass go-kart BMW!"

"Hey V! I'm going about 70 right now. So I'm going to slow down to about 60, then I'm going to need you to tuck and roll."

"Stupid," Devon snapped back. "How does that make sense, being that I'm in the backseat of a coupe? Dumbass."

"Wait, wait, back up. What's with the whole single-letter thing?" Simone inquired.

"It's something we've been doing since we were kids," I explained as I flipped Devon off. "Since our names both start with the same letter, it was hard for the neighborhood kids to get our names right. So, we came up with Z and V."

Devon popped his head from the back seat and said, "And they still got it wrong."

When I pulled into my apartment complex, Devon said his goodbyes, jumped in his car, and drove off. I stood there with Simone, feeling nervous. I didn't want to bring her home, and now that she was here, I just wanted to call her an Uber.

I think she sensed my nervousness because she walked over to me and kissed my bottom lip. "Are you going to invite me in?"

"Uh, yeah. I'm sorry. I mean, if you don't want to—"

She hushed me with a finger to my lips and slowly, yet deliberately, ran her other hand over my print, whispering, "I'm very sure of what I want." And with that, despite my best intentions, my old demons resurfaced.

From where we were standing, my first-floor apartment was a straight shot. Simone and I walked passionately to my apartment, pausing every few steps to kiss. As soon as we got to my door, I picked Simone up and pressed her against the wall, shielding us from any potentially watching neighbors. I live in a relatively safe neighborhood where even white women feel secure enough to walk their dogs at night. Nevertheless, I didn't want anyone getting a free show.

Her breathing was unsteady as I kissed her neck. She hiked up her dress, and my fingers found her panties. I rubbed her as our kisses deepened with lustful passion. Simone grew more intimate and ready. I tugged her panties aside as if I were about to take her right there, but she patted my chest and shook her head. I let her down gently, trying to regain my composure. Her face was a mixture of surprise and embarrassment as she caught her breath. Seeing her want me so intensely only fueled my desire further. I put my key in the lock and opened the door before my lust overwhelmed me again. As we walked into the still-lit room, I slowed the pace by asking her what she thought of Devon.

"I like him," she said, adjusting her dress.

"Yeah, blood couldn't make us closer." I watched her as she surveyed my sparsely furnished bachelor apartment. It was a humble abode—just a plush couch, a mounted TV, an entertainment center, and a coffee table—none of which matched. The place lacked decorations, sticking to essentials only.

"What? Not what you were expecting?" I asked, a hint of sarcasm in my voice.

"I'm sorry." She looked almost embarrassed. "When I saw you walk into the club, I thought you could buy me a drink. You should have saved your money and let me buy you one." She smiled.

"Oh, you're so freaking funny. As you must know, I spend most of my time at work, so I only use this place to sleep, especially in my amazing bed. I hope that's okay with you."

"I'm okay with you showing me where your bathroom is so I can pee."

"Oh wow, is your mouth always that vulgar?" I smiled, pointing to the closed bathroom door. She rolled her eyes and flicked me off.

While she was in the bathroom, I tried to make sense of the night. Something felt off. I've had women approach me before, but with her, it felt like she targeted me. Maybe I'm overthinking it. We had a genuine conversation, and it felt natural, like I wanted to know her more. It was eerily similar to when I met Gianna. Why am I comparing her to Gianna? Especially since I don't really know this Simone at all. I don't even know if Simone is her real name. There are plenty of women who know me only as Christian.

"DENZEL!!!"

I snapped out of my trance. My thoughts had been so loud I hadn't noticed Simone standing in front of me, completely naked. As I returned to reality, I took in her long, slender chocolate legs crossed over each other, her dark nipples suspended in the air, and her curly dreadlocks cascading down to her breasts.

"Uh, yeah. Hey, hey," I stuttered.

"Hey? I was expecting more than that. But it's cute because you sound like a college virgin."

"I'm sorry, I just didn't expect you to come out looking so—"

"Naked?"

"Naked." I repeated, the words tumbling awkwardly from my mouth.

She slowly walked toward me, her breasts bouncing in rhythm with each stride as if she moved in slow motion. I took in every inch of her body, imagining the taste of her skin. The intensity of the moment overcame me. I met her halfway, lifted her, and wrapped her legs around my waist. I started to lay her on the carpet, but she whispered, "No, take me to the bed you love so much." I hoisted her back up over my shoulder, kicked the slightly ajar door to the dark bedroom open wider, and tossed her onto the bed. Watching her land among the pillows, she playfully grabbed one and threw it at me. I blocked it easily and smiled down at her.

The moonlight glimmered on her skin as I removed my shirt. She opened her legs and began touching herself, moaning softly. I unzipped my pants, releasing my rock-hard erection, all the while watching her moisten my sheets.

I knew I was making a mistake, but I couldn't resist. "Simone will be the last one," I thought. "She has to be because I can't keep living like this. Plus, it's not like it'll kill me." So, I mounted her to test our connection. A moment of ecstasy washed over me as I entered, and then a sudden, painful prick on my backside jolted me. I pushed up to climb off her, but my arms gave out, then my consciousness faded into darkness.

CHAPTER 3

A DREAM PT. I

I AWOKE, RESISTING THE urge to open my eyes. For a brief moment, the darkness was comforting. Yet, the sunshine, radiant and insistent, pried my eyelids open. The brightness told me it was Sunday. Since childhood, I'd noticed Sundays always seemed sunnier, as if God wanted to ensure no one had an excuse to sleep in and miss church. Beside me, Simone slept peacefully. I gave her a soft kiss on the cheek, a sweet gesture with a hidden agenda. I needed her awake and out soon. She looked too comfortable, and I was running late to take my grandmother to church.

"Hey, I have to take my grandma to church," I whispered.

"Okay, have fun. I'll wait for you here," Simone mumbled sleepily.

"You think I'm going to leave you in my apartment while I take my grandma to a Black church? You're funny. It's okay. I'll call you later."

"Why should I leave?" Simone protested, sitting up and clutching the comforter for modesty. "I don't have anything planned, and I'm curious to see if sober Denzel and Saturday night Denzel are two different people."

"First off, there are two sides to every coin."

"Yeah, and you're a cornball in daylight, too. So, what's the second point?" she teased.

"What second point?"

"You said 'first off.' You can't say that without a follow-up. Otherwise, you look silly," Simone said, laughing.

"Wait, I look silly? We just had sex, Simone. I've seen you naked. Why are you hiding behind the comforter?"

"I can't believe I just had sex with you," she said, touching her forehead in mock despair. "Do you even know anything about women?"

"Look, I'm not a gynecologist. I don't study the vagina; I just know to make it feel good," I retorted, my tone soft yet firm.

"Oh my God! There's no way I could date someone like you. You think you're so hilarious." She exclaimed, half amused and half exasperated.

"I'm the corny, funny type. I'm the closest thing you're going to get to Will Smith. So, you're welcome," I laughed.

"Will Smith? If only you looked like him, then it would've been perfect."

I gave her a blank, sarcastic face. "There's something different about you. I can't put my finger on it," I said.

"Let me guess; I'm unlike any woman you've ever met," she replied, climbing out of the bed to stretch. Her dreadlocks cascaded down to the small of her back. I couldn't help but stare at her magnificent body, contemplating a re-encounter. As she lowered her arms and spun to face me, her breasts bounced softly. She was beautiful—her body, her smile.

"For someone who was in such a rush to take their grandmother to church, you sure are taking your time staring at me," she said, slipping into her dress from the previous night.

"I can't even pretend I wasn't looking. You might be the most beautiful woman I've ever seen."

"Is it just corny line after corny line with you? Guys swear they're different, but you all sound the same."

"Well, I don't have any experience with horny guys, but I can assure you I'm just as corny with all my other friends as well. That's what makes me different. I embrace my corniness."

Simone walked to the bedroom door, typing something on her phone. She leaned against the door and sighed. "You're more similar than you think. Different wrapping paper, but the same gift."

She opened the door and left the bedroom. I pulled on my boxers and followed her to the living room. Leaning against the wall next to her, I asked, "Meaning?"

"In my experience," she said, her back against the front door, "guys do what they need to get the woman they're pursuing. Whether it's being the funny guy, the Mr. Fix It, or the bad boy we want but don't need. Men only play the role that's needed for sex. But what role do women play?"

I paused, expecting her to continue.

"That's an actual question, Denzel. What role do we have in these little schemes you men play?"

I wanted to give an answer that would stump her, but I had nothing.

When I shrugged my shoulders, she answered, "Saying yes. No matter how you present yourself or how funny you are, it all means nothing unless we want it as well. So, the chase men love is nothing more than a false perception of the control we give you."

I was in complete awe. My mouth felt like it was stuck open. "You used me."

"And you played your role as planned, baby," she laughed, blew me a kiss, and then turned and walked out of the apartment. I stood there, dumbfounded. I had never let someone get the upper hand on me before today, which surprisingly made me smile.

After picking up my grandmother, I sat in the pew, listening to the pastor preach about choices, prompting me to reflect on my life. Simone was one of many women I had woken up next to, knowing their bodies but not them. How many women had I hurt because Simone was right? Having chased countless women, pretending to be someone else and promising I was different, only to leave them in the same place of hurt as many before me. I might be like every other man, or perhaps something even worse.

Just at the peak of my epiphany, Grandma Pearl flicked my ear, making it feel like it was about to fly off.

"Denzel Eugene Williams. If you don't get out of your thoughts and listen to the pastor!" she whispered forcefully. "I will still take you to the bathroom and wear you out."

"Did it ever occur to you I might be having a revelation of my own? That my silence is a good thing?" I whispered back.

She reared her head back and said, "No, because considering how late you picked me up this morning, your revelation is probably something nasty. Now hush and listen to this man preach!"

I immediately corrected my posture and focused on the pastor. However, my mind could not stop dwelling on Simone until the church service was over. After the service, which was usually my favorite part of going to church—when the entire congregation would mingle, hug, and chat like a family catching up—it felt different this Sunday. Grandma held my arm and said, "Come on, take me home, Denzel."

"Are you sure, Grandma? I mean, don't you—"

Mid-sentence, she turned towards the doors and walked out of the church building. Something seemed off. She was colder than before. I rushed out of the church doors and saw her halfway to my car. Once I caught up, I opened the door for her. She didn't even glance at me as she got in. I had never seen her this quiet or reserved. Normally, during the long drive home after church, she would use the time to give me a personal come-to-Jesus message telling me about my potential and how God has a purpose for it. But today, she sat mute, staring out the window as I drove.

"What's going on with you? You're never this quiet," I asked.

"Boy, if I wanted to talk, I would talk. I am 75 years old and have been talking longer than you've been breathing," she snapped back, rolling her neck.

"Okay, fine, but it's going to be a long, silent ride. You know I don't have any Mighty Clouds of Joy in my music library," I said, hoping to coax a smile, a laugh, or some sign of happiness. But she remained unresponsive. As I drove, I glanced at her every few seconds, trying to make eye contact. If I couldn't be anything else, I could at least be annoying.

"What, boy!?" she snapped.

"Grandma, I'm not about to just sit here and listen to you breathe." She gave me the death stare. "Look, I'm sorry. I'm just worried about you because you're not acting like yourself."

She leaned against the door to face me. For a long while, she stared at me, unblinking and unmoving.

"Grandma Pearl, you're looking at me like Ali looked at that one boxer who called him Cassius," I tried again, hoping to lighten the mood.

She sat forward in her seat and said, "Do you know what today is?"

"Yeah, it's Sunday. We just came from church service."

"You always have to be the funniest man in the room," she snapped. "It's June 14th, the anniversary of your mother's death. And you're walking around cracking jokes like everything is one big fucking joke!"

"Whoa, whoa, Grandma. I'm sorry, I forgot it was today. I don't usually make a big deal out of these things."

When we pulled up to her driveway, I turned the car off. I knew that this conversation was just beginning.

"Denzel, why don't you like to think about her death? I've been waiting for this conversation since you were a teenager. I saw you struggling with it, and it was too painful back then, so I put it off. Then your life took off, and I didn't think I needed to bring it up, but you're falling to a rock bottom that I don't want for you."

"Just because I don't remember her death on purpose doesn't mean I'm almost at rock bottom. I mean, it's not like I don't think about her; I do a lot."

"Denzel, baby, I know you think about her because there isn't a day that goes by that I don't either. But your issue isn't her memory. Your issue is letting her go."

"What do you mean? I know she's not here. Grandma, I don't know what you're getting at, but I am not heading for rock bottom. My job at the hospital is going great, and I have a lot of money saved. I don't drink unless it's social and sure, I might smoke a little weed, but you know that. Other than that, I'm good, besides my student loan debt."

"You think you are so smart, Denzel. You've figured out all the loopholes in life and have scapegoats on retainer, but you're still afraid to face the bigger issue, baby."

"What's the bigger issue?"

"You're afraid to let anyone close to you because you never want to risk losing someone again. So, you keep people at a distance, and you manipulate and scheme to get what you want. You push away anyone who could love you for the person you are."

"Look, Grandma," I tried to comfort her. "If I lost you, it would be depressing, but just like Mom, you'd be watching over me. So, I know I'm not alone. Plus, I think you're forgetting about Gianna. She is the one who loves me for who I am. That's why I'm marrying her. Speaking of, I would love to continue this conversation, but I have to pick her up from the airport soon. The email from her command said they should be landing soon, and I want—"

"Yeah, okay. Perfect timing, I guess," she said to my grinning face. "We're not done with this talk. Tell my future granddaughter that I'm glad she made it back safe from deployment and that I love her and want to see her."

"That was a lot of stuff you listed, Grandma, but I think I can remember all of it."

"Shut up, boy!" she said as she opened the door. "Denzel, baby, one other thing. Please don't let Gianna see these panties on your floor. Now, come over here and help me out of this car.

You know I raised you better than this. I ought to knock you out."

Embarrassed, I hurried to the other side of the car to assist her. She smacked the back of my head—a mix of chastisement and pent-up aggression. After I walked Grandma Pearl to her door, her words resonated with me. Was I deflecting my fear of abandonment by pushing love away?

I returned to the car and immediately dismissed the thought. I noticed the panties casually dropped on the ground and smiled, appreciating Simone's cunning. It impressed me even more to think she managed to take them off unnoticed with another person in the car. The sexiest asset a woman has is her brain, and Simone certainly knew how to use hers. I picked up the panties, stuffed them into my pocket, placed my car key fob on top to keep them secure, and then drove off to the airport.

Devon's call rang through my car speakers as I merged onto the interstate. "What up, V?"

"Denzel, Mr. Steal Your Girl! Yo, have you added those panties to the chandelier yet? She was bad."

"It's funny you ask because I have them on me right now," I chuckled.

"What did you say? My guy, I knew you were into some weird shit, but are you wearing panties now? And didn't you take your grandma to church this morning? You're a nasty mother—!"

"Shut up! They're in my pocket, fool!"

"But you still took them to church, though?"

"I can't do this with you. I'm on my way to pick up Gianna now, and you're distracting me."

"I swear I want to be like you when I grow up. You wife up a military chick and have the full white picket fence dream house. Even with all that, you still run your game through all the seven cities when she's on deployment."

"Aren't you the one always at my throat for saying way too much on the phone?"

"Yeah, but the FBI ain't looking for you because you're just a cheater," he laughed.

I hung up the phone, trying my hardest not to lose focus. I reverted my brain back to being the lucky husband and made my way to the airport entrance. Pulling into the lane for arriving flights, I veered past the waiting traffic and headed straight for the employee parking. I rolled my window down to the toll booth worker, a burly black man with an enormous stomach and an even more massive grey beard. I gave him a nod as I eased to a stop and asked, "Hey, my man, is Jayla here? I'm dropping off her medication."

"Yeah, she's here," he said, looking over his shoulder for her. "Hold on. Don't move."

I pulled down my visor and opened my mirror to get a good look at my wavy black hair and decided I needed a quick once-over. I pulled up the cover to my armrest compartment, where I kept my essentials, and grabbed my brush. From a distance, I heard a woman's voice yell, "Shut up, Donald!" There wasn't enough time to brush my hair, so I threw the brush back inside the armrest and turned my flirting switch back on. I saw Jayla walking toward me on my left, and I slouched in my seat as if I was sleeping.

"Z, I know you're not sleeping. Donald told me you just pulled up," she said, sticking her arm through my open window and mushing her hand in my face.

"Damn, Gina, why do you have to do all that?"

"Boy, you ain't no Martin, and I know I look better than Gina, so who are you trying to play? Get out of the car and hug me. I haven't seen you in a long time."

I unlatched my seat belt, stepped out of the car, and leaned on the door after shutting it. She leaned in and wrapped her arms around my neck, her long black hair entangling itself in my beard. I kissed and nibbled on her neck just enough to make her squeal.

She pushed herself off me, slapped me on the chest, and said, "You play too much, Z. Why are you starting something you know you ain't going to finish?"

"Who said I wasn't trying to finish?"

"Boy, please," she said. "I ain't had a night out with you since you met Gianna. You meet a light-skinned girl and forget all about me."

"Jayla, I just gave you head last weekend."

"Yeah, but you completely ignored the fact I brought up Gianna. It's cool. I know where I stand."

"If you don't stop playing with me like you're not married. Anyway, speaking of Gianna..."

"Yeah, yeah, yeah. You need a place to park while you pick her up, don't you?"

"You know me better than I know myself, baby."

"Please, Z, nobody really knows you, but I got you."

"Thank you, sweetheart. Come here," I said, wrapping one arm around her waist and pulling her closer. I lifted her chin and kissed her hard, probably too passionately for that parking space, but it was a spur-of-the-moment thing. At the end of our kiss, I bit her bottom lip.

"You and this biting isn't fair," she moaned.

"Why not? It's fun because I love seeing your smile when I do it," I said, wiping her lip gloss off my lips.

"You know that turns me on, and you keep doing it. Now I'm going to be sitting in this booth with soaked panties because of you."

"Since when do you wear panties?"

"Boy, get in your car before I punch you in the face," she said, turning and smiling.

"Alright, where do you want me to park?"

"Park next to my car, right here," she said, lifting the garage barrier and pointing to her black Altima behind the gate.

After I parked, I took a moment to prepare myself before seeing Gianna again. I slapped my cheeks lightly, took a deep breath, and tried to slip back into the mentality of the honorable man of the house. It's always easy for me to make the switch. Hopefully, one day, I won't have to anymore. I stepped out of my car and walked to the Arrival entrance.

CHAPTER 4

A DREAM PT. 2

RIDING UP THE ESCALATOR, I felt myself getting a little giddy at the prospect of seeing Gianna again. When I reached the top, I saw the food court with the departure sign straight ahead and the arrivals sign to my right. Looking down at the Arrival section, I noticed several families with banners and posters from her division. I sat on a bench by myself and reached into my pocket to get my phone, scrolling through social media to pass the time.

While sitting, I looked up and saw an exhausted, pregnant mother at her wit's end. Her two young children were running, screaming, knocking down displays, and licking random glass panes. The mother seemed to have no energy to chase them around the food court. I realized I was staring, but I couldn't look away. The little boy was chasing the girl around a garbage can, and then she took off and jumped over a small bench. Instinctively, the little boy copied her and leaped after his sister. As he was about to land, the little girl drew back her hand and smacked him hard. I looked at the mother, who was on her feet, waddling and yelling, "Wait until your father gets here. You guys are going to get it."

I let out a small chuckle, covered by a cough, and turned my eyes back to my cell phone. Those kids must have been a handful over the past six months. I wouldn't have come home if I were the father of those little terrors.

I stood up to see if anyone knew any information about the flight. I scanned the food court and spotted a guy sitting at one of the red leather stools in a vintage 1950s-style bar at the heart of the food court. He seemed to be part of my group, given the poster curled up in the seat beside him, and best of all, he had no kids. So, I approached him and asked, "Hey, my man, do you know exactly when the flight is coming in?"

He looked at me, took one earbud out, and said sternly, "The email said 4:00 pm." He then put the earbud back in and returned his gaze to what I could now see was a half-full glass of dark liquor.

Typically, I would have responded with a similarly curt remark, but this guy looked like he was trying to numb himself. He had that intense look of someone expecting a brawl. So, I wisely moved to the opposite side of the bar and sat down on a stool. I checked my watch at 3:30. The bartender immediately noticed my abrupt seating and spun a napkin on the checkered bar top.

"I take it you want something strong like his," he said in a raspy Southern drawl, nodding toward Mr. Angry Earbuds.

"Um, no. I'm not that upset with my life. Give me your favorite lager," I replied with a chuckle.

"You got it, Doc."

As he poured my beer, he kept glancing at the other side of the bar, checking if the coast was clear. "You know," he started softly, "he hasn't taken one sip of that drink. He's just been sitting there staring at it. I don't know if he's being frugal or saving it for just before his wife arrives."

I looked to my right and saw the guy staring at the bottom of his glass, spinning it on its napkin. "I've been there before," I said, turning back to the bartender. "It's the last of his freedom liquor he's trying to cherish."

I took my credit card out of my wallet to pay, but the bartender held up his hand, stopping me.

"Been there too. This one's on me, Doc," he said, tapping his knuckles on the bar counter. I tipped my head and raised my glass to him. As I hoped, the bartender let me enjoy the last moments of freedom alone. I sat there, sipping and watching the sports highlights on the television, when I heard a familiar voice call my name.

"Denzel? Denzel, what are you doing here?"

I turned around to see Tara with a pleasantly surprised expression. She was pushing an all-black baby stroller with its hood down and a blue and white striped blanket covering what appeared to be a child. I nearly choked on my beer when I saw her. I had never imagined I would run into her here, especially with Gianna due to arrive at any minute.

"Tara, what are you doing here?"

"I know, right?" she said, her smile gleaming. "I flew back to Virginia to see you and ran into you at the airport five minutes after I got off my plane. What are the odds, right?"

"Probably as much as finding shit in a snowstorm," I mumbled. "Why were you planning to see me?" I asked in a normal voice before taking another sip of my beer.

"Oh, I wanted you to meet your son."

I spit the beer out onto the bar top at her sudden revelation. "Wait, you were still preg..."

"Everything alright, son?" the bartender interrupted, having walked down to wipe up my spill. The timing of his urgency suggested he was close by to hear details.

"Uh, yeah," I said, picking up a napkin to wipe my mouth. I turned my back to the bartender and pulled Tara in close. "Tara, what do you mean? That's my child?"

Tara stepped back to pull the blanket off, revealing the child. I stood up and saw a blonde, blue-eyed baby staring at me. "Doesn't he look exactly like you?" she said, looking at the baby proudly.

"What the hell do you mean, exactly like me? That baby has blue eyes. Both of our eyes are brown."

"What are you talking about, silly? He has our eyes."

"Are you delusional? You can't tell me this little blond-haired, blue-eyed baby is mine. Look at him." I looked back down at the baby to provide proof of my claim. But staring back at me was a dark, curly-haired child with beautiful brown eyes, smiling at me. I was speechless. I scanned the room to see if I was being pranked because there was no way this baby had transformed into another race.

"So, Denzel, will you pick your son up?" Tara said, pushing the stroller closer to me.

It took me a few seconds to register that Tara spoke to me. My mind couldn't stop reeling over how the baby's eyes had shifted from blue to brown in mere seconds.

"Hello?" Tara prompted, trying to snap me out of my trance. "Are you going to pick up your son? I flew all this way because he needs you in his life."

It was almost as if Tara wasn't speaking English. I watched her mouth move, but my brain couldn't make sense of her words. I glanced at the baby again to see if its appearance had changed, but its brown eyes met mine with the same joyous expression.

"Look, Tara, you couldn't have come at a worse time. My fiancée is about to walk through those arrival doors at any moment. The last thing I need is for her to see me with you and a baby," I said.

"Your fiancée?!" Tara's tone shifted from joyful to incredulous.

"Yes, my fiancée. We've been through..."

Before I could finish, Tara slapped me across the cheek. The force was more powerful than I anticipated, causing me to stumble onto the bar top and knock my beer over on the service side. The bartender was quick to intervene, trying to calm Tara down. I saw this as an opportunity to make an escape. Gianna could not find me here, arguing with a woman and a baby she claimed was mine.

Anticipating my exit, I slowly edged toward Mr. Angry Ear Buds. As Tara's voice escalated into a yell and she pushed over the bar's garnish tray, I seized my chance and bolted around the opposite side of the bar toward the men's bathroom. I waited until 4:00 pm, periodically peeking out to see if Tara was still at the bar. Cracking the door open, I heard no trace of her, nor did I see anyone at the bar. I stepped out further to catch the bartender's eye. He only took a few seconds to notice and wave me out, signaling that the coast was clear.

"Hey man, I'm sorry about that," I said, approaching the bar. "I didn't know she would be here, let alone go ballistic like that."

"Look, Doc, these deployment pickups are always filled with drama. There's always a baby mama or an estranged girlfriend popping up. I didn't expect her to slap you, though. But I'll tell you, that little lady is much stronger than she looks," the bartender commented.

"What happened to Mr. Angry?" I asked, changing the subject.

"Oh, he left about five minutes ago with his family. I would have come to get you, but I didn't know you were waiting for the same flight."

"It's fine. I don't know why Gi wouldn't call or text me," I said, waking up my phone. Unfortunately, I only saw the wallpaper photo of Gianna accepting my marriage proposal. I unlocked my phone and called her, only to reach her voicemail. "Damn!" I grunted.

"Your woman went AWOL on you, huh?" the bartender remarked, tossing his bar towel over his shoulder. "Probably a good thing because God only knows what the other girl would have done if they'd met."

I didn't even acknowledge his comment. Instead, my thoughts remained fixated on Gianna and why I hadn't heard from her. In a panic, I rushed out of the food court and saw that the crowd of families outside the arrival gate had dispersed. Desperate, I sprinted to the airport's front doors, hoping Gianna would be outside waiting for me with a mischievous smirk, telling me it was all a joke. I walked through the front doors and saw nothing but families embracing their long-awaited loved ones. I pulled out my cell phone again to call Gianna. There was a pause for a few seconds, then, "Hey, it's Gianna. Leave a message..."

I hung up in frustration, panicking and running my hands through my hair. At that moment, every irrational thought I could muster flooded my brain. First, I thought about Gianna's hospital being under attack, leaving no survivors. But that wouldn't make sense because I would have heard something on the news. Then I wondered if she was missing in action. Finally, in a last moment of despair, I turned toward the end of the welcome home caravan and saw a woman in uniform getting into the front seat of an SUV while a tall man leaned heavily on the trunk to close it.

I ran to flag them down before they could pull away. Frantically knocking on the passenger window, the woman turned around in shock. Her husband walked around to the passenger side, understandably confused. "Excuse me, ma'am. I'm sorry to frighten you, but I'm looking for my fiancée. She was supposed to return today, but I haven't seen her."

"Oh no, I'm sorry, hun," the woman said. "What's her name?"

"Snyder, Gianna Snyder, ma'am."

"No, I don't know anyone by that name. What detachment was she with?"

"I honestly wish I could tell you, ma'am, but I can't understand most of what she tells me. But I know she's a physician who worked at the hospital over there."

"Oh, I'm sorry. I don't know, then. We were the last battalion out of there. Divisions were shipping out all weekend, so she might have returned earlier than expected. So many divisions were involved in this deployment; there's no way all of them could return today alone."

"That must be it. Thank you for your time," I said, slightly annoyed by the lack of information, though it wasn't her fault she didn't know Gianna. Before Gianna left, she had told me that if she landed earlier than expected, she would give me a heads-up. I waited until I saw the line of returning veterans thin out before I felt comfortable enough to leave. As I stood there and watched the cars depart one by one, I called Gianna a dozen more times. Still, with no answer, I headed back to my car. Maybe she had headed home. Either way, this was different from the welcome home I was expecting.

CHAPTER 5
A DREAM PT. 3

DRIVING EASTBOUND DOWN I-264 was stressful enough without the added worry that the love of my life might be missing. Typically, the traffic clogged the lanes with drivers who were either too timid or overly bold about speeding. I found myself caught in the frustrating muddle of the former. The constant stop-and-go was exhausting. It was a tiresome cycle of halting and inching forward for twenty minutes, each pause punctuated by the threat of rear-ending the car in front. Finally, my patience snapped. I slammed my hand against the scorching steering wheel as traffic ground to a halt.

"This is just perfect!" I yelled.

An interstate transformed into a parking lot was the last thing I needed. I exhaled a long sigh, shifted my car into park, and fished for my phone in my pocket. I needed music—any kind would do—to distract me from spiraling thoughts. Yet, as I scrolled through my playlists, my mind was consumed with thoughts of Gianna. Where could she be? She was supposed to be at the airport. We had planned this meticulously, and Gianna was always one to stick to plans. Could she have left me?

Tears welled up in my eyes as I remembered what today represented. It had been twenty-eight years since I lost my mother. Now, it seemed fate might be echoing that loss with Gianna. Gianna, who inspired me to be a better man, who was everything I never dared hope for in a partner. Now, I couldn't find her, and panic was setting in. What if she had been killed in action? I wasn't even home to receive that devastating knock at the door. What would I have done if I had been home? I remember being there when Grandma Pearl received my mom's flag. I've never had to bear the heavy fold of that flag myself. I've never felt that soul-crushing weight as the fabric settled in my hands.

Suddenly, a distant siren wailed from behind. I scanned my mirrors to discern if the emergency lights were yellow or blue. Yellow typically signaled a roadside assistance vehicle that could do little until a state trooper arrived with their blue lights. But the lights flashing through the traffic were blue, followed by a cascade of red and white. Instantly, a state trooper and a convoy of fire engines sped past in the emergency lane. Watching the emergency vehicles disappear, I noticed a plume of black smoke rising into the sky.

"What the hell is going on?" I mumbled.

Following the example set by many others, I exited my car to see what was causing the commotion. The crowd sauntered toward the smoke, and as we approached a bend, the source of the smoke became visible—flames leaping into the air. Suddenly, the faint screams of pain reached my ears, growing more apparent and more distinct as we neared. They were the screams of children. Initially moving with curiosity toward the accident, the crowd surged forward in a panicked rush toward the cries.

Rounding the bend, I saw a school bus on its side, engulfed in flames. Children struggled to escape through the windows. An explosion at the front of the bus sent a funnel of fire into the air like a roaring dragon. The horrific sight rooted me to the spot. Trauma is my job, my passion, but in that moment, my body froze. All I could do was stand and watch as people rushed past me towards the bus.

"Get those people out of here!" someone yelled.

"Ladies and gentlemen!" a state trooper called out from his patrol car, his voice booming through a megaphone. "Please return to your vehicles. This area is too dangerous. I repeat, return to your vehicles."

Like mindless drones, the crowd and I returned to our cars while firefighters doused the bus with water. The walk back wasn't enough to erase the horror I had just witnessed. Once I settled back into my car, traffic flowed as if the accident had never happened. Driving past the site, there was no sign of the burning bus or the children. Before long, the disturbing thoughts of burning children faded into the soul-shattering panic of possibly finding an empty home. I sped home, hoping, praying Gianna was there.

Each second passed like minutes as I sped through the main road of my neighborhood. Thoughts played like movies in my mind. My world slowed until I turned down my street and saw my white colonial-style house. As I passed my neighbor's massive hedge, I spotted Gianna's white Pathfinder parked in our driveway. I remembered the moment I bought her the car, her face when she saw it on Christmas morning, and when I saw it in my rearview mirror six months ago as I drove her to the airport.

I pulled in behind her car slowly. My hand trembled as I took it off the gearshift; I clasped it with the other hand to steady it. My breaths were shallow and erratic, my anxiety too high to walk through the front door. I popped open my glove compartment and reached for one of the mini bottles of whiskey I kept for emergencies. I cracked open the whiskey and poured it down my throat, the burn of the alcohol traveling to my belly but also filling me with a sign of fleeting courage. I opened my car door and stepped out, hoping the calm would last.

Walking across our front lawn, I saw the honey-oak chairs on the porch, rocking gently in the soft June evening breeze. Climbing the porch steps, I glanced at the chairs and remembered the laughs we had shared on them. My trembles worsened as I extended my key to the front door. I steadied my hand and slid the key into the lock. The heavy lock clicked open. Anticipation tightened my throat. I paused to take one final deep breath before opening the door.

Inside the house, sunlight peeking through the blinds illuminated the foyer. The place was quiet, almost deserted. I glanced into the living room to my right and noticed dust accumulating on the table. Having not returned since I took Gianna to the airport, I recalled her first deployment when we moved in together. I used to clean every Sunday, afraid of what she might think. By her second deployment, I had reduced my efforts to every other month. Now, during her third, I hadn't cleaned at all.

The click of a lighter snapped me out of my reverie, signaling I wasn't alone. A strong aroma of tobacco followed the sound. It couldn't be Gianna; she doesn't smoke. So, who was in my house? And how long had they been here?

I slowly crept backward, my hand stretched wide, reaching for the bat I kept by the door. My fingers found the familiar hard maple, and I quietly grasped its handle. My heartbeat surged, pulsating through every inch of me as the scent of a burning cigarette grew stronger. I followed the smoke through the dining room to the kitchen. With my back pressed against the wall leading into the kitchen, I took a deep breath, tightened my sweaty grip on the bat, and rounded the corner, ready to confront the intruder.

As my eyes focused on the figure sitting in the kitchen corner, relief washed over me—it was Gianna.

She was seated at the kitchen table, dressed in one of my T-shirts and a pair of cotton boxers, and with her back to the patio door. Despite my intention to startle her, she remained motionless, her legs crossed, one arm resting on the glass table with a cigarette between her fingers, and her other hand drawing patterns around something on the table. The kitchen island obscured my view, so I had to tread cautiously.

"Babe, oh my God, you scared the shit out of me!" I exclaimed in relief, dropping the bat by the refrigerator.

"Yeah, I can tell," she said, eyeing the bat as it clunked on the tile floor and rolled under the refrigerator.

"Why weren't you at the airport? I was going crazy looking for you," I asked as I walked deeper into our spacious kitchen toward her.

"Don't take another step," Gianna said, calm but firm as I reached the island.

"What do you mean? I haven't seen you in six months. Hell, I thought you were dead. There's no way you're keeping me from hugging you and giving you all this love," I joked, walking around the island with my arms outstretched, beckoning her.

The object Gianna had been tracing with her finger became more evident as I drew closer. I saw the handle of her service pistol, her hand hovering over the short but prominent muzzle pointed in my direction. I halted immediately, my words and fear caught in my throat. Remaining ever so calm, Gianna took another drag of her cigarette and exhaled the smoke in my direction.

"When did you, um, start smoking cigarettes?" I asked cautiously.

"Out of everything around you, that's where you want to focus? The cigarette?" Her voice was tinged with irritation.

"To be perfectly honest, not really. But I'm kind of panicking right now," I replied, my voice cracking.

"What day is it?" Gianna asked, taking another drag from her cigarette. She locked her eyes with mine, making it feel like a trap—a question women ask when they already have damning proof but are baiting men into lying.

"What?" I stuttered.

"What day is it, Denzel?" She repeated, pointing to the calendar behind me with her cigarette hand. I slowly turned my head and saw a red circle around June 14th. "It's June 14th."

Gianna took another drag and breathlessly said, "No, it's not. It's Sunday." She exhaled smoke in my direction again. "How long have I been here?" she asked, her voice taking on a menacing tone.

"I don't know. That's what scared me because we were supposed to meet at the airport, but I couldn't find you," I said, my gaze fixed on the gun barrel resting on the table.

"Denzel, do you want to know what I admire about you?" Gianna asked, picking up her service pistol and examining it as though admiring the finality of its function.

"I am so confused about where this is going, so no, I don't," I admitted nervously.

"Even when staring at death, you never drop the act," she said, placing the gun back on the table.

"What act?" I instinctively asked. I couldn't fathom what she meant. I sifted through my mind, searching for any hint of her accusations. The only thing I could think of was losing her on the anniversary of my mother's death. "Gi," I said, "let's be rational. I honestly don't know what you mean. My only focus has been finding you. You know today is the anniversary of my mother's death. When I didn't see you at the airport, all I could think about was losing you the same way I lost her."

Gianna's stern expression slowly cracked into a smile, and she began to clap slowly. She took one last drag of her cigarette and stubbed it on the glass table. "I asked you how long I have been here. Since that question, nothing but bullshit has come out of your mouth," Gianna said, standing up and grabbing the gun off the table, initially pointing it at the floor. She then raised the weapon, stepped forward, and relaxed her shoulders. This crazy woman was assuming her shooting stance.

"Now, how long have I been here? And before you answer, think. Think about the position you're in and the position I'm in. Literal or figurative, take your pick, but give me any more bullshit and—" she said, cocking the gun.

"I, uh, don't... I mean, I don't know how long you've been here. How long has it been?" I managed, trying desperately not to panic.

"Excellent, Denzel," Gianna said as she sat back down, presenting me with her profile. She laid the gun on the table, the barrel still pointing in my direction. "I've been here for two days, Denzel."

"Two days?!" The words escaped my mouth before I could catch them. After my outburst, she shot a sharp glance back at me. I raised my hands and took a few steps back.

Gianna shifted her gaze away and continued, "Two days I've been here, and I haven't seen or heard from you. I could ask you where you've been, but even with lying clearly being the wrong choice, I know you'd still choose it. So, asking you would waste both my time and yours. I could guess, but no." She paused. "What fun would that be? We both know what you've been doing since I left."

"Fun?!" I exclaimed. "This is supposed to be fun for you?"

"Why can't it be? I mean, you had six months to have your fun. Do you want to know what I did for fun these last six months?"

"I can only imagine. You were away for a long time, and God only knows the conditions you had to endure. It was a long six months for both of us. I can't blame you for what you did or wanted to do."

Gianna let out a sinister laugh. "You are a fucking genius. I mean, in an oblivious way, but still a genius. You deflect but speak as though you've solved the problem when you are the problem," she chuckled again. "It's one of the traits about you, Denzel, that I will miss."

I backpedaled out of the kitchen toward the dining room and asked, "What do you mean, 'going to miss'?"

Gianna stood up, matching my pace with her charcoal grey .45mm swaying. She pointed at the ground and said, "You are a master at deflecting. After we met, I realized that was part of your personality, but the levels you've taken to are beyond what I expected." Gianna raised the gun and aimed it at my chest as I reached behind me, groping for the handle of the baseball bat. Then she fired a warning shot into the refrigerator.

"No, no, no, no. You're going to pay for your sins." She motioned me out to the living room.

Gianna followed, keeping the sights of her gun trained on me. "I was excited, you know. I wanted to come home and surprise you. I needed this surprise because this last tour was the hardest. I've done things I'm not proud of to get back to you. I've killed to get back to you." A tear formed in the corner of her eye and trickled down to her chin. "I get it, though. It's my fault. I trusted a snake but was surprised it bit me."

"Look, Gi," I started.

"No!" Gianna interrupted sharply. "It's not your turn to talk. If you could, you would talk your way out of anything. But that's not going to happen today. Today, you will pay for your constant hurt and disrespect towards me. You have broken me, built me up, and broken me down so many times that I don't even know who I am anymore. To find myself again, I must lose you."

My eyes widened as I gazed at the tip of the barrel pointed at me. With sweat beading on my forehead, I begged for my life.

"Gianna, I'm sorry, I'm horrible. I don't deserve you or anyone, but I deserve my life. It's my fault; I treated you terribly." I fell to my hands and knees, bowing toward her feet. "Gianna, you can be happier with someone else. Killing me may seem worth it, but you will destroy your life. Don't give up your life because of how I treated you. I still love you, and that love will torment me for the rest of my life. Let me carry this grief and shame. You are blameless, but you won't be anymore if you pull that trigger." I raised my head, hoping she would see the shame in my eyes, but when I looked up, I was alone. Gianna had vanished.

Where did she go? I spun around, half-expecting her to circle behind me like a predator. Surprisingly, I was still alone, kneeling in our living room. I rose to my feet and began searching for her, starting in the kitchen where I had first encountered her anger. The chair Gianna had sat in was pushed in neatly, and aside from the dust that had accumulated, it was clean of any ashes or stray cigarette butts. The smell of smoke had vanished entirely as well. It was as if Gianna had never been here, much like the bus accident earlier.

Running frantically, I searched upstairs to see if she had gone to pack her things. As I dashed around the house, I pondered the irony of searching for someone who wanted me dead. Yet, I continued to search, finding no sign that Gianna had ever been there. Every inch of the house remained untouched. Her clothes still hung opposite mine in our walk-in closet. Her toothbrush, jewelry, and extensive collection of shoes were all in the same places she'd left them when she shipped out.

I patted myself down, searched for my phone, and realized it wasn't in my pocket. I retraced my steps in my head for likely places my phone might be and then realized I had never taken it out of the car. I darted for the stairs, reached the bottom with one gigantic leap, and sprinted to my car door.

Approaching my car, I saw the light from my phone screen and heard the faint tones of my ringer. I swung open the door just as the sound died, and my phone went black. Waking my lock screen, I saw seven missed calls from Grandma Pearl's cell phone. A notification for a voicemail appeared on my screen, and I sat in the front seat to listen.

"Good evening, Mr. Williams. I am Roger Harris, an EMT at Saint Paul's Immaculate Hospital. Due to privacy regulations, I cannot disclose the details of this call. However, Mrs. Anita Pearl Williams listed you as her emergency contact, and it is imperative that you return my call promptly. I will be using your grandmother's phone. Please call me as soon as possible."

I ended the voicemail and dialed my grandmother's number. The phone rang briefly before I heard the same burly voice answer, "This is EMT Roger Harris answering for Mrs. Williams."

"Yes, this is Denzel Williams, Anita Williams' grandson," I said, trying to keep my voice steady.

"Sir, could you please provide her date of birth? I need to verify that you know the patient," he requested.

"Didn't you just leave me a voicemail?" I asked, my voice rising slightly in frustration. "I apologize. I didn't mean to raise my voice. Today hasn't been the best day, and now I'm receiving this call."

"Sir, I completely understand and want to give you all the information I can. However, I can't legally disclose it over the phone unless I have verification that you know the patient," he explained.

"No, I'm a doctor, so I understand the protocol. Her birthday is March 6th, 1943," I said, providing the necessary information.

"Thank you, Mr. Williams. Unfortunately, your grandmother is here in the ICU at Saint Paul's," he began.

"What happened?" I inquired anxiously.

"Well, we aren't entirely sure now," he continued. "We responded to a rescue call at her residence. When we arrived, she was found lying unconscious in the kitchen. There was a small fire on the stove. We believe she might have been cooking when she fell. Fortunately, we arrived in time to prevent the fire from spreading to the rest of the house. We've admitted her for minimal smoke inhalation, but she still has not regained consciousness, and we are still investigating the cause."

"Okay, I'm in my car right now, and I will be there as fast as possible," I said, closing my door and starting the engine. I hung up the phone and put the car in reverse. It was rude to cut off the EMT so abruptly, but given everything that happened today, this is a far worse feeling than I could have imagined. The mental replays of burning children, the fear of losing Gianna morphing into the fear of my own death, could all be bearable. But the thought of losing Grandmother Pearl—that might just be my breaking point.

CHAPTER 6

A DREAM PT. 4

MY DRIVE TO THE hospital was much smoother than my tumultuous encounter with Gianna's rage. Heading westbound to downtown Norfolk, all I could think about was how badly I'd messed up. My eyes teared up as the fear of losing Grandma Pearl overwhelmed me. With sorrow streaming down my face, I sped toward Hospital's Corner.

Hospital's Corner is home to three major hospitals in this area of Virginia. First, there's Saint Joseph's Children's Hospital and Trauma Center, where I work. Next is the Naval Hospital, tucked in the back of the medical cul-de-sac. Then there's Saint Paul's Hospital — the state's largest and most well-funded hospital, known for attracting many bright minds annually. Typically, the thought of this place fills me with joy, anticipating new experiences. But today, I want to turn my car around and drive far away. Pulling into the parking garage, I didn't even think to check my glove compartment for another mini-bottle of whiskey. No amount of alcohol could make this any easier.

Walking into Saint Paul's ER, the admittance line nearly reached the front sliding doors. I bypassed the long line and noticed a woman, crying frantically, dash past the security guard into the patient area. The guard quickly jumped to his feet and chased after her. Looking around, the waiting room was packed with families showing the same raw emotion as the frantic woman, likely relatives of the school bus accident victims.

Turning back to the desk, I saw a young black nurse assisting a patient from what appeared to be a vital signs room. I approached her. "Excuse me, ma'am, can you help me?"

"Sir," she stated, without eye contact, "you can't just walk in here and get seen without signing in first."

"Excuse me, Nurse... what is your name?" I asked sternly.

"Jasmine," she replied, finally meeting my gaze.

"Hi Jasmine, let's start over before I speak with your director. My name is Dr. Denzel Williams, and I am the attending surgeon at Saint Joseph's, right across the parking lot. I'm not a patient. My grandmother is in the ICU, and I need to know her room number."

Her expression shifted from dismissive to embarrassed. "I'm so sorry, Dr. Williams. It's been a terrible day. I'm not sure of her exact room, but our ICU is on the 6th floor," she explained, pointing to the elevators around the corner.

Without another word, I turned and headed for the elevator to the ICU. The doors opened, and I stepped out, feeling like my heart had sunk to my feet. Around the corner was the nurses' station, but I hesitated, not ready to face another tragedy. Yet, despite my reluctance, thinking of Grandma Pearl lying there alone spurred me on.

"Excuse me," I said to a blonde nurse behind the desk, looking down at the paperwork. "I'm looking for my grandmother, Anita Williams."

She looked up, her crystal blue eyes sparking a flicker of recognition. "Mr. Williams, we've been trying to reach you for a while," she said, standing to shake my hand. "Your grandmother is in severe condition."

"How bad is it?" I asked, my voice tense.

"Let's talk over here," she suggested, guiding me to a seating area. I settled onto a blue leather couch near the entry, and she pulled a rolling stool from under an end table and placed it in front of me.

"Mr. Williams," she began, her gaze intense and sympathetic. "I should wait for her physician to return, but there might not be enough time. Your grandmother's condition is unusual. As you know, she was involved in a small house fire. She passed out while cooking, but we're still unsure why. While on oxygen in the ER, she suddenly crashed—I mean, her condition rapidly deteriorated."

"Ma'am, I am a physician myself. I understand that means she went into cardiac arrest," I said, hanging my head, struggling to hold back tears.

"Oh, okay. I can speak more straightforwardly, then. When Mrs. Williams arrived, she was alert and oriented, with stable vitals and blood flow. All signs pointed to her being discharged in the morning after observation. However, she became unresponsive when we attempted to contact you. Initially, we thought it might be an embolism, so we started treatment with blood thinners, but..."

I waved my hand to interrupt her. "Ma'am, all of this is important, but it's not what I need right now. I don't mean to be disrespectful, but I need to be with my grandmother," I said, rising to my feet. The nurse grabbed my wrist as I turned to leave the seating area, her expression showing she was holding back tears herself.

"Mr. Williams, I haven't told you the strange part yet. Every time her heart stopped, it only happened when we tried contacting you. As soon as the EMT hung up, her heart rhythm normalized, as if nothing had happened."

"I'm confused," I said, sitting back down, my brow furrowed. "What does that have to do with me being in the room?"

"Our theory is, the closer you are to her, the closer she gets to death. It sounds like fiction, but it's the only explanation that makes sense," she said, holding onto my arm.

"So you're telling me that the only way to keep my grandmother alive is to stay away from her?" I asked, pulling my arm away. "That sounds like the biggest nonsense I've ever heard. No offense."

"Mr. Williams, I understand how absurd this sounds, and if I were in your position, nobody could stop me from seeing my loved one. But the reality we're facing is real, and keeping her alive means maintaining your distance for now. At least until we can figure this out. I know it's an impossible request, but it's necessary."

"Look, I appreciate everything you are doing to save my grandmother, but if you think I'm just going to sit around and not see the closest thing I have to a mother, you're mistaken," I said, standing once more. She reached for my arm again to stop me. I pulled away sharply this time, leaving her standing there, hand to her mouth.

Exiting the seating area, I turned left to search every room number for a placard labeled A. Williams. The first four rooms were vacant, with neatly made hospital beds and patient supplies on the end tables. I continued to search the rest of the rooms in the ward. The deeper I ventured into the ward, the more I heard the random beeping from the monitors in each room. One beeping cadence was slightly more distinct than the others but sounded even more distant. Turning a corner, I was between rooms 608 and 609, and the beeping grew louder. Instinct told me to follow the beep. The closer I walked, the louder and faster the beeping became, as if a homing beacon was engaging me. Finally, I stopped in front of room 613, where the beeping ceased its pulsing melody and transitioned into a long-drawn tone. Curious, I turned to investigate the room. Through the sliding doors, I could see light protruding through the closed curtains. I pulled the doors apart and snatched open the curtains. An elderly white woman jumped in her bed and screamed.

"I am so sorry, Mrs..." I peeked back out of the room to check her placard. Blanchard, I was looking for my grandmother. I'm very sorry to have startled you."

Before Mrs. Blanchard could respond, I heard what sounded like a freight train of people storming into the room next door. Peering through the cracks in the glass windows, I saw a crash cart and a room full of medical staff.

"Oh, that's okay, sweetie. When you find her, come back and visit. It's not every day I wake up to someone as handsome as you in my room," Mrs. Blanchard said, winking at me. I gave a nervous smile and backed out of the room. As I moved into the main walkway, I accidentally collided with the blonde, blue-eyed nurse.

"I am so sorry. I should have been looking where I was going," I said, helping the fallen nurse.

"Oh no, it's fine," she replied, focusing not on me but on the room full of people next to Mrs. Blanchard's room.

She walked to the sliding doors and entered the chaotic scene in the room. I glanced at the placard, which read Room 614: A. Williams. My heart sank. Was that nurse right? Did I cause my grandmother's decline by ignoring her warning? If I entered her room, could I make things worse? Overwhelmed, I sat behind the adjacent nurses' station desk, too afraid to leave and even more afraid to enter the room.

While I sat behind the nurse's station, I felt every second pass. I focused on the moving sneakers under her room's dark green floral curtains. I was utterly useless, debilitated by fear, and paralyzed by the shame I brought to those I claimed to love.

The chaos eventually subsided, and the scuff of sneakers all became still. I sat up sharply, anticipating the facial expression of the first person to emerge from the room. The curtain split open from the middle just enough for a white hand to poke through. The person stood still before coming out as if gathering himself. When he appeared fully from behind the curtain, I saw it was an older gentleman with a thick grey mustache, putting on his white lab coat. His face looked drawn. He scanned the area behind the nurse's station and finally made eye contact with me. The contact lasted only a second before his eyes shifted to the floor as he walked toward me. That look told me everything I needed to know without a word being spoken. My head dropped as my worst fears became reality. Every woman I ever loved was now gone from me forever.

He approached and asked, "Mr. Williams?"

"Yeah," I said, my gaze still fixed on the patterns of the carpeted floor.

"We tried everything possible, but your grandmother didn't make it. I am so sorry for your loss. The nurse mentioned you were over at Saint Joseph's after you guys had spoken. If there's anything you need..."

I shook my head, never looking up. Although I focused on the floor as he spoke, the room seemed to swirl around me. His voice came through, muffled and slow.

I wasn't sure when the doctor left, but I soon realized I was alone. The company of white coats had disappeared, too. The room was empty, except for my grandmother's lifeless body.

"Are you going to see her?" a voice said behind me. I spun around and saw the blonde, blue-eyed nurse sitting on the counter beside the medication dispenser.

"How long have you been sitting there?" I asked, wiping my teary eyes with my fingers.

"Long enough to comfort, but not so long that it became creepy," she replied, smiling. The nurse jumped down from the counter, and I noticed two paper cups filled with something dark behind her. She handed me one of the cups and offered, "Coffee?"

"Sure, but I will need something much stronger than this." I sipped the black coffee, and the back of my mouth stung with the taste of whiskey. I looked up at her, surprised by her gesture.

"I lost my mom around this time last year, so I know what you're going through," she said, pulling up a chair to sit beside me. "When she passed, I didn't want anyone to speak to me because there was nothing they could do."

"Tell me about it. I appreciate your company, really. It's just that this isn't my first rodeo. My mom passed when I was ten, and now my second mom when I'm 38," I said, pulling my cup to my lips to take another sip.

"Hey," she said, raising her cup, "to our moms." We clinked our paper cups with a soft thud and sipped. "So, Mr. Williams..."

I interrupted. "No, call me Denzel. That's the least you can do."

"Okay, Denzel. Are you going in to see her?"

I paused and stared at Grandma Pearl's room, trying to weigh the reasons for seeing her. "No, there's nothing for me to see but her body. She's not there anymore, and seeing her like that would just break my heart."

"I get it. I really do. I didn't want to see my mom, not even at the funeral. I prayed it was all just a dream and that I would wake up."

I looked at my coffee as I swirled it in my cup. "Yeah, I wish it were. That woman has been everything to me since my mother died," I said, leaning back in my chair and propping my feet up on the counter. "I remember back in high school, I was dating this girl named Keisha. We lived down the street from each other, and the entire neighborhood would have planned our wedding if they could." The nurse chuckled. "I'm serious. People saw us as the perfect couple. Then, one day, I met a girl at the mall with my best friend, Devon. I brought her back home while my grandmother was working. What I didn't know was that Grandma Pearl didn't have to work that day. She only went out shopping and had lunch with a friend. So Grandma Pearl walked in on me on top of this girl. Oh my God, she was so pissed."

The nurse leaned forward on the edge of her seat. "And she kicked your ass, didn't she?

"Actually, no. Grandma Pearl knew I was having sex. What she didn't like was the cheating. It just so happens that Keisha was the friend Grandma Pearl had been hanging out with all day. And she happened to be downstairs in the kitchen putting away the groceries."

"No way," she said, leaning back in her chair.

"I swear. Grandma Pearl took Keisha under her wing while she was growing up. You'd think she would've kicked the girl I brought home out by her hair. Instead, she looked at her and said, 'Sweetie, I don't know your name, but if you want to leave this house safely, you wait until Keisha is gone.' Then she turned to me and said, 'Denzel, go take Keisha for a walk, tell her the truth, and break up with her. She's too precious to deserve how you're treating her.'"

"Oh my God. This lady was a saint. I don't know how you're still alive after that. So, what happened with Keisha? Did you tell her the truth?" she asked, chuckling.

"Hell, no!" I laughed. "I lied my ass off, and Grandma Pearl knew it. She never mentioned it again, though." We both laughed as we finished our cups of coffee. "How did you know I worked at Saint Joseph's? I only told you I was a physician."

She stood up and said, "Well, you're the one who announced it in the whole ED waiting room. You should know how hospitals gossip."

I stood up and said, "I didn't realize I was that loud."

"You weren't, but the nurse called the floor and let us know an asshole doctor from Saint Joseph's was on his way and to tread carefully."

"Yeah, I was an asshole. But hey, thank you for sitting with me. I needed it."

"No problem, Denzel. I, uh, have to give some meds," she said, looking at her watch.

"No, go ahead. I'm going to go home and get some rest," I replied, checking my watch and noting it was half past midnight.

Driving back home, I felt somewhat uplifted by that nurse. Something about her was so calming and sweet. It made processing everything somehow easier. But that ease disappeared when I pulled into my driveway and saw the front door cracked open. I rushed into the house and found it ransacked. Drawers were pulled out and scattered on our kitchen, bedroom, and bathroom floor. Did I not lock the doors? I thought, retracing my steps. That's when I noticed that all my things were untouched. The only items missing from the house were Gianna's.

I dragged myself to the kitchen to see if she had also taken the bottles of alcohol. True to form, every single one was gone, except my aged whiskey. The bottle was still there, but it looked like Gianna had hit it against the counter before leaving. A pile of glass dust lay on the marble countertops, and shards sprinkled on the tiles below. I inspected the bottle, trying to salvage the liquor, and sure enough, chipped glass floated at the bottom.

Gianna knew I would come to my one refuge and didn't shy away from trying to hurt me. Staring at the glass shards floating in the liquor, I reached for the mesh strainer hanging over the island. I filtered my aged whiskey into a glass and tossed the colander into the sink.

I sat in the same seat at the table where Gianna had confronted me. Glancing down at my watch, it read 1:13 am. I took a big gulp of whiskey. My panic eased, replaced by anger. It was the kind of rage I had always feared to unleash. Memories of laughter, arguments, and love flashed through my mind as I stared around the house, fueling my fury.

When my anger peaked, I rolled the Louisville Slugger from under the refrigerator. I placed my glass on the kitchen island and gripped the bat with both hands. My rage intensified as I stared at the bat until I had to release it. I put the bat to everything I could find—mirrors, TVs, dishes all felt my wrath. It was relieving at first until the room spun. My knees went limp, and I lost my balance, crashing down onto the shards of glass on the floor.

I wasn't sure if it was the whiskey or if I was losing my mind, but it felt like someone had yanked me by the navel through the floor. My world went black. I tried to compose myself, but my body felt numb. Panic set in. My breathing became difficult to control, and then, nothing.

CHAPTER 7
THE AWAKENING

I WOKE UP WITH a jolt of pain, struggling to open my eyes as if they had been glued shut. My entire body tingled with numbness and piercing hot pins and needles. Suddenly, the pain concentrated in my abdomen—it felt like someone had clenched my intestines, squeezing and twisting them relentlessly. My throat began to tighten and moisten; I knew I was going to vomit, whether I wanted to or not. My only hope was to make it to the toilet in time. I leaped out of bed and dashed to my master bathroom. The first bit of puke splashed the bathtub, but I got the rest into the toilet.

After my stomach emptied, I lay face down on the cool tile, clutching my stomach in pain. As the room spun, I couldn't help but wonder what had happened to me. I remembered Grandma Pearl dying.

"What the hell?!" I screamed, trying to reach for my cell phone to call her. I attempted to jump to my feet, but my legs, gelatin-like, collapsed beneath me, sending me crashing onto the tile floor face-first. My head thumping, I army crawled back to my bed when a flashback of Gianna seared into my memory. We were back at our house, which made little sense because she had left me when I proposed. A person doesn't forget pain like that, yet the pain I felt yesterday was more vivid than the memory of Gianna walking away. The fear of her pulling the gun on me, the emptiness I felt when Grandma Pearl died—my brain insisted it was all real. But was it? Could I have been hallucinating? Is it even possible to do so while dreaming?

I reached onto my bed and felt under the pillow, still afraid to use my legs. My fingertips brushed the cold surface of my phone screen. But something else was there, too. I flung the pillow off the bed with a sweep of my arm, revealing what felt like a post-it note. I pulled it down to see what it said:

"I tried to wake you before leaving, but you were sleeping like a rock. I had fun last night, and I'm glad you gave in to me. XOXO - Simone."

I balled up the note and tossed it over my shoulder. I grabbed my phone to see I had missed four calls from my grandmother, one missed call, and six texts from Devon. I decided to call Grandma Pearl first; I needed to make sure she was okay. I laid on the floor beside the bed and listened as her line trilled. It took a while, but she finally picked up.

"Hey, boo bear," she said, her voice instantly calming me. It was light and joyful, nothing like in my dream.

"Hey, Grandma. You don't know how happy I am to hear your voice," I said, pressing my hand against my forehead.

"Well, I'm happy to hear from you too, baby, even though you forgot about me," she said, her tone tinged with disappointment. Flashes from my dream came back to me—the curtains of her hospital room and the flatline tone of the monitor.

"Huh, um," I stuttered, trying to compose myself. "What do you mean, forgot about you?"

"You were supposed to pick me up for church and never showed. So I called you, but I figured you were tired from your shift and were sleeping."

"Grandma, this is going to sound crazy. But, in my mind, I picked you up yesterday, and you ended up dying," I said, my eyes welling up with tears.

"Oh, baby, that was nothing but a dream. I'm alright."

"That's the thing, Grandma, it didn't feel like one. It all felt too real. I feel like I'm losing my mind. I just had a flash of the dream, making me feel like I'm still caught up in it."

"Oh, baby, it was just a nightmare. Are you still taking your medication?"

"Yes, ma'am, but it's not the meds. I've never experienced anything like this before. It wasn't just a normal nightmare. I can remember every moment as if it really happened."

"What do you mean?" she asked.

"You know when you're dreaming, and it feels like you're going through all the motions, like a character in a movie? But, when you wake up, you forget almost everything except bits and pieces."

"Yeah."

"Well, it's hard to explain, but this was nothing like that. I can remember everything and still feel every emotion. All the hurt and panic I felt is still with me."

"You're just tired, baby. You work hard, and your body is telling you to get more sleep."

"Grandma, I was sleeping. That's when I had the dream. I even took a two-hour nap before going out with Devon after finishing a normal 12-hour shift at seven o'clock. Not to mention the 8 or 9 hours of sleep the day before."

"Mmmm-hmmm. I know you, boy. There's no way on God's green earth you're getting 8 hours of sleep, especially with your mother's death anniversary. And I know you're still dealing with what happened with Gianna. Tell the truth, boy, are you taking drugs? It sounds like you're on acid."

"No, Grandma, I'm not on acid. I'm trying to explain, but it's difficult," I sighed.

"I hear you trying, baby, but I don't understand. What I do know is you didn't take me to church yesterday. So, I had to call that fool Devon to come and get me."

"Wait. What? Hold on." I went to check the messages Devon had sent me. They read:

7:02 a.m.: Yooo Z, how freaky did you get last night? She seemed like a handful, in all sense of the word.

8:16 a.m.: Ms. Pearl just called me to take her to church. Where you at? I didn't want to spend my last Sunday off in church.

10:04 a.m.: We just sat down. This better not take all morning. Hit me back, bro. I know you're not still with that girl.

"Grandma, this doesn't make sense. What day is it?" I asked her. Before she could answer, my phone alarm went off, signaling it was time for work.

"It's Monday, baby. That's what I meant when I said you forgot me for church. Why don't you know what day it is? Is it because of the acid?"

"Hey, Grandma, I'm going to call you later. I have to get ready for work," I said, rushing her off the phone. I needed to contemplate how I had just missed an entire day. I hung up and checked the date on my phone's home screen: Monday, June 15th. But how? How is it already Monday? I'm losing my mind.

I rolled over to see if I could stand. When I pushed off the floor, my legs seemed sturdy enough. However, as I rose, my head felt too heavy for my neck. The room tilted, and I stumbled against the wall. Regaining my balance, I walked into the bathroom, turned on the shower, and rinsed the dried vomit off the wall.

When the tub was clean, I stood under the warm water, letting it cascade down the back of my head. I felt the streams of water glide down my beard, watching drops fall from my chin as I spoke to myself, trying to distinguish what was real from what was not.

No matter how hard I thought about it, I couldn't shake everything from my dream. How could I remember it all? Simone, in the morning, attended church with Grandma, waited for Gianna at the airport, and was surprised by Tara—it all seemed too real. Real enough, that Sunday completely disappeared from me. "How did I pee?" I asked myself as I turned off the shower. I left the bathroom, letting the water trails linger on my skin in the coolness of my bedroom.

My brain felt like it was splitting in half. On one side, I convinced myself it was a dream. But I couldn't shake the panic and the trauma I felt. I could curl up in bed and cry all day just thinking about Grandma Pearl's death, even though I had just spoken with her. Then, as I walked into my closet to get dressed, a text arrived on my phone. I rushed over and saw it was from Grandma Pearl.

"Hey baby, I was thinking about what you said, and maybe you need to see someone to talk this out."

Of course, she would think that. Before I could reply, I noticed my phone's display read 6:24 a.m.

"Oh crap, I'm going to be late," I muttered, dropping my phone back on the bed. I threw on some workout clothes and rushed to my car. As I started the engine, I reached into my pocket for my phone but found it empty. I must have left it on the bed. Cursing, I pushed the car door open and returned to grab it. There, I noticed a balled-up post-it note on the floor. Thoughts of Simone and precisely what happened on Saturday swirled in my mind as my phone vibrated on my comforter—it was Devon.

"Just the person I wanted to talk to," I said, answering the phone.

"My sentiments exactly. Look, at least let me know the next time you want to ditch church duty with Mrs. Pearl. The man didn't preach until he heard 4 hours of songs. I thought I was a hostage. And you didn't even bother to text me back."

"There's a reason for that. I think I spent all Sunday in bed. Hold on, my phone is switching to the car," I said, backing out of my parking space. "Hey V, you still there?"

"Hell yeah, I'm still here. You owe me, man. I was trapped in church for like 8 hours because of you."

"Look, V, I don't have time for jokes. I'm late for work, and I had the craziest day of my life that I have to tell you about."

"How did you have the craziest day if you were in bed? Wait, don't answer that. You took that dread-headed girl home. I don't want to know."

"Okay, so you saw me take her home then," I said, a note of satisfaction in my voice.

"What do you mean?" He asked, needing clarification. "I had to climb in the back of your BMW and listen to your corny ass the entire ride home. You sounded like you fell in love."

"Simone is the reason I wanted to talk to you. I needed to verify that it was real and not a hallucination. So, it was only just Sunday."

"Hallucination, what did y'all take, bath salts?"

"Honestly, I wouldn't rule anything out the way I'm feeling right now."

"Z, bro, I'm lost. It's kinda simple. Either you were on bath salts, or you weren't."

"Look, after you left, I took her to the apartment. I remember she came out of the bathroom naked, and we went into my room. Then I remember nothing except waking up on what I thought was Sunday. Simone got dressed, and I took Grandma to church."

"No, you didn't," Devon said, sighing.

"That's why I feel crazy; in my mind, I did. And after church, I went to the airport to pick up Gianna from her deployment."

"Hold on," he cut me off again, "Gianna, Gianna? The same girl who left you looking stupid at that French restaurant after you proposed? That Gianna?"

"Yeah, the heartbreaker."

"So now you're having dreams about it too?" he said, holding back his laughter.

"Yeah," I said, ignoring his attempt to make light of the situation. "I was supposed to pick Gianna up at the airport. But she wasn't there, so I returned to our old house. She was there waiting for me, smoking a cigarette. She looked strange as if she wasn't all there mentally. Then she told me she knew I was cheating, picked up her service pistol, and aimed it at my head. I closed my eyes to beg for my life, and when I opened them, she was gone."

"What do you mean, 'gone'?"

"She was gone, like not in the house anymore. So, of course, I'm wondering what's going on. I tried to call her, but before I could, I received a voicemail from an EMT over at Saint Paul's saying Grandma Pearl was dying, and I couldn't see her before she passed."

"Man, this sounds like a typical nightmare," he said.

"That's what Grandma Pearl said, but this nightmare seemed to last all day, and I remember every detail. To top it all off, I don't think I left my bed on Sunday. I think I slept through the whole day. That's why I didn't take Grandma Pearl to church or respond to your texts and calls."

"What are you saying? You slept for over 24 hours? I hate to break it to you, but that's impossible."

"That's the only explanation that makes sense because I didn't hear your calls and don't remember what happened yesterday."

"Well, answer me this. How did you pee? You couldn't have held it all day."

"Your guess is as good as mine. When I woke up, I didn't even need to go. The only weird thing was my stomach was killing me, but I threw up, and it eventually went away."

There was a slight pause. I patiently waited for Devon to say something as I took the exit towards Hospital's Corner. "Are you still there?" I asked.

"Yeah, I'm just thinking. It sounds like a bad dream, but you don't sound like yourself, so it must be real to you. Do you think the dread-headed girl did something to you?"

"The thought crossed my mind right before you called, but she left me a post-it note saying she tried to wake me up and none of my stuff was missing. Plus, I didn't leave her alone long enough for her to drug my drink all night."

"You are the hardest person to wake in the world. I don't know, man. It sounds like you need to talk to someone about this."

"Yeah, that's the same thing Grandma Pearl suggested," I said, pulling into the employee parking garage and exiting my car.

"For real? I'm surprised she didn't tell you to anoint your house and start fasting," he said, chuckling.

"Right. But look, I just parked, and I have to make rounds. So, what time are you coming in?" I asked.

"I'm supposed to be there at 8, but I'm going to tell them I slept past my alarm, so I'll be in around 9:30, 10-ish."

"I don't know how you don't get fired. You act like I didn't get you this job."

"I told you, I have my supervisor in my back pocket. So, for the time being, I'm good," he laughed.

"Well, on your way in, pick me up some coffee. I didn't have time this morning."

"Do I look like your servant? Plus, you owe me, fool."

"Man, have my coffee ready!" I yelled, hanging up the phone before walking through the sliding doors of St. Peter's.

CHAPTER 8

A DREAM COME TO LIFE

TALKING WITH DEVON ALWAYS eased my spirit. I found solace in the familiarity of our conversations, drawing comfort from yesterday's experiences, still shrouded in mystery but allowing me to focus on the day ahead. Approaching the hospital front desk, I greeted Mrs. Pat with a genuine smile, knowing she was always a welcoming presence.

I've known Mrs. Pat since I started working here. Despite her age, she appeared perennially youthful, a 60-year-old woman who could easily pass for 40. She was not just a colleague but also my closest female friend at work, privy to every morsel of gossip that circulated through the hospital—a confidante whose loyalty was preferable to the alternative.

"Hey, Dr. Williams, with your fine self," she drawled, elongating the sentence teasingly, fully aware of my discomfort with compliments. It was a dynamic between us—more sarcasm than genuine admiration.

"Mrs. Pat, must we go through this every time?" I sighed, approaching her desk and leaning in. The familiar banter brought a sense of routine to the morning. "Why must you torment me so?"

"Why, whatever do you mean, sir?" she replied, feigning innocence, leaning back in her chair and placing a hand on her chest in mock astonishment. "I'm simply wishing the finest doctor this side of the Mississippi a good morning."

"What's the latest gossip? You always have something up your sleeve," I said, glancing at my phone discreetly. Mrs. Pat had a knack for prolonging conversations longer than necessary.

"Late for rounds, aren't you?" she chuckled knowingly, deflecting my inquiry with practiced ease.

"Well, I can always spare a moment for my favorite gossipmonger. So, what's the scoop this time?"

"Well..." she began, glancing cautiously around as if checking for eavesdroppers. "I heard things are getting serious between you and Nurse Ashley in ortho," she whispered conspiratorially, leaning closer.

"Oh, Mrs. Pat. Your little birdies aren't singing the right tune. That ship sailed last year, and I cut ties with her when Gianna left."

"How are you doing with that, anyway? Are you still locked up in your apartment?"

"Well, you know how much I love my bed," I laughed. "But thanks for always checking in on me. You've always got my back."

"Yeah, more than these doctors here," she said, glancing at her ringing phone. Holding up a finger, she reached for the receiver.

I knew this was my cue to escape. Motioning to my phone, I mouthed, "I gotta go."

I headed to the elevators and clicked the up button, ruminating on my reputation in this hospital. I wasn't the esteemed doctor on the fast track to promotion; I was merely fodder for their entertainment—a reality show of heartaches and mistakes.

As the doors opened, I stepped in, rubbing my face with my palm. Just as the doors started to close, a voice yelled from a distance, "Can you hold that, please?" Putting my hand on the elevator door, I peeked to see who was coming. It was Andrea, a nurse from my department.

Andrea was the name I expected Mrs. Pat to say. We'd started seeing each other a couple of weeks ago, nothing serious enough for titles, but we hung out now and then. She was fun to be around, with a pleasant, kind personality.

Andrea ran around the corner and into the elevator, her blonde hair tied up in a messy bun that looked professionally done. Her crystal blue eyes seemed to sparkle as she made eye contact with me. "Oh, it's you," she said, rolling her beautiful eyes.

"It's me?!" I scrunched up my face. "I'm not sure if I should be offended or offended," I said as the doors closed again.

"You should be offended because you didn't text me all weekend," she said, leaning against the opposite wall.

"I'm sorry; this weekend was kind of crazy."

"Oh, crazy, huh? What, did you get confused about which slut you were entertaining?"

"You sound jealous," I said, walking toward her slowly.

"Denzel, stop," she said, extending her hand to keep me at bay. "I'm not going to have sex with you in an elevator."

I backed up. "Yeah, that's not smart. It's not like we're the only people here." She gave me a disgusted look and rolled her eyes again. I wiped my mouth and said, "You're right. I'm sorry; that was too much. After you clock in, come to my office, and I can give you a proper apology."

"So, you think you can leave me waiting by the phone all weekend, and I'm just supposed to run back to your arms?" she said, folding her arms across her chest and cocking her head to the side.

"Well," I started, "if you were waiting by the phone all weekend, that tells me you probably want me more than you are mad at me right now."

"Oh, my fucking God! You are so arrogant." The elevator doors opened to an empty hallway.

"But am I right?" I asked with a grin. "After you."

She exited the elevator and turned left toward the staff lounge while I turned right toward my office. Stopping and turning around, I glanced at her as she walked away in her scrubs. Andrea preemptively turned around as well. Our eyes met, and I winked; I could see her smirk as she turned around. When I turned around, I had a flashback to the kind nurse in my dream, seeing her blue eyes and blonde hair in a ponytail.

"Was that Andrea?" I whispered, feeling my chest tighten as the room swirled again. Leaning against the wall, I could feel beads of sweat forming on my forehead.

Why was she in my dream? Why didn't I recognize her? What does all this mean? My colleague, Dr. McAvoy, interrupted my thoughts, rounding the corner from his office. He shot me a pretentious glance from head to toe and sniggered.

"You're late, Dr. Williams!" he declared, looming over me.

Dan McAvoy stood about my height but was much skinnier, sporting thick glasses. He exuded an air of thinness and clumsiness, the archetype of a snobby genius doctor. We have known each other since our undergraduate days. If ever there was an opposing equal, it was him. He possessed the innate intelligence I wished I had. While I spent days studying to maintain my B average, Dan merely glanced at his study material to dominate the class. Yet, I had social skills with patients and women that he could never acquire.

"Yeah, and I'm pretty sure you're still a virgin, Dan," I retorted, straightening up and wiping sweat from my forehead.

"Denzel, perhaps you forgot I am married," Dan replied arrogantly.

"I know you're married. That's what makes it so funny," I said, proudly laughing in Dan's face.

Dan scoffed. "Rounds start in 10 minutes."

"Then I'll see you in about 15," I heard Dan murmur under his breath as I turned toward my office. His opinion mattered little to me.

Finally reaching my office, I closed the door with relief. Flashes of Andrea from my dream lingered. Settling into my red leather Chesterfield-style chair, I leaned back, struggling to recall the nurse's face from my dream. I could only grasp her hair and eyes; her face remained blurred. Was it Andrea? She was the sole source of comfort in the dream if it was a dream at all. A soft knock on my office door interrupted my thoughts once more.

"Yeah," I replied, wishing whoever it was would disappear. A young, timid male intern tentatively cracked open the door, barely revealing his face. All I could discern was a shiny forehead and black hair buzzed short. His faint, quivering voice reached me, "Dr. Williams, we are ready to conduct rounds."

"Damn, son, am I a villain or something? You can open the door," I said in exasperation. He apologized and closed the door. Clapping my hand against my forehead, dragging it down my face. I won't make it if Devon doesn't hurry with my coffee.

Walking onto the Pediatric ICU floor, I noticed an unusual absence of commotion. The ward was never this quiet. Approaching the nurse's station, I asked Andrea how many patients we had on the floor.

"We have four patients so far, Dr. Williams," she said, smiling.

I rubbed my eyebrows in frustration. "Is that it?"

"Look, you may like a busy day, but a low patient load makes for a relaxing 12 hours for the rest of us," she replied.

"Long and boring is the perfect day for you," I quipped as the residents and interns gathered behind the nurse's station. "You know I like it fast-paced and noisy." Winking at her, I walked off.

"Alright, people," I said, making my way through the middle of the semicircle. "I'm looking at my watch, and it's about 7:30, so lay it on me. Who's first?" I shouted to the tired and nervous staff.

"Could you be any less professional?" Dan said, emerging from the workroom behind me.

"I mean, I could, but your wife would think less of me." I turned around immediately and saw Dan's face turn red. "I'm kidding, Dan. Calm down. She's not real." The circle erupted with laughter, everyone except Dan.

I scanned the circle and saw the same buzz-cut intern toward the back and pointed for him to come forward. He slowly walked around his colleagues to the front, holding his notes in his trembling hands. "What's your name, son?" I asked.

"Daniel, sir. Daniel Choi," he said, staring at the floor.

"Dan, the intern, Dr. Dan, all we're missing is a lieutenant, and we'll have a band," I said, grinning at Dr. McEvoy. He returned my mockery with a grimace. I turned back to Daniel. "What do we have, Mr. Choi?"

"We have four patients on the floor, sir. The first patient is Isaiah Fuller, a three-week-old who came into the ER with labored breathing late last night. The patient was premature and diagnosed with respiratory distress syndrome at birth. We intubated him around 3 am last night. Airway levels are all normal. He has an umbilical line and is on a normal saline drip. Plans to transfer him to the NICU will be coordinated this morning."

"Alright, excellent, Daniel. Now, who's next?" I asked, scanning the semicircle of nervous faces. "You," I said, pointing to the red-haired female intern looking down at her notes. "What's your name?"

She looked surprised, as expected. "Ummm, Amy, sir." She paused like she wasn't sure what came next until I egged her with my hand for her to continue.

"Oh, yes, umm, Tyler, our fifteen-month-old failure to thrive. He is a pre-admit for a G-tube placement. He has been a hard stick for blood draws because of prenatal exposure to heroin, so his veins are fragile. Nutrition and GI are picking up his treatment following his discharge." With a deep breath, Amy dropped her head back down to her notes to follow along.

"Very good, a little dramatic, but it's Monday. Alright, and the next one?" I asked. Amy was so unaware that I was still speaking to her that the room fell into an awkward silence. Not until a colleague nudged her did Amy look up again.

"Oh, I'm sorry, I thought, umm, give me a second," Amy said, flipping her folded stack of notes back and forth. "Yes. Hannah Goldstein, our three-year-old VIP. Her parents are on the board of directors, and she presented to the ER with nasal obstruction to the left nostril. During the examination, we discovered a bead stuck in her..." Amy briefly paused to check her notes, "right nostril. The bead, unfortunately, could not be retrieved at the bedside, so she went to the OR late last night with success in the retrieval. She is currently awaiting discharge."

"Beautiful Amy, I'll stop picking on you now," I laughed. The group chuckled, and Amy grinned, happily stepping back. "Alright, that's three, and I'm guessing that the last patient is Steven Waterman, correct?"

"Yes, sir," Daniel said, proudly stepping to the front of the crowd.

"This is the problem with your jokes," Dr. McEvoy sneered, staring at Daniel. "The people who need to be studying are too busy laughing. It gives them false confidence that they will graduate from the program."

"I'm not sure what you mean, sir?" Daniel said, crawling back into his shell.

"Don't mind him, Daniel," I said reassuringly. "Go on."

"Well, Dr. Williams, Steven originally came in for jaundice and pain. His pain level is tolerable with meds, and his updated liver functioning labs look golden."

"Golden?" I asked, raising my eyebrow. "What does that mean, Daniel?"

"Oh, um, just a figure of speech, sir."

"So, his lab values are baseline?" Daniel nodded. "Okay, let's keep the communication simple to eliminate confusion." I winked and held my fist out for a fist bump. Daniel bumped my fist and smiled. "Alright, people, it looks like we have an easy day, so let's keep it that way."

The huddle of exhausted residents broke. Some headed to the locker rooms, while others went to their computers to start their shifts. As they dispersed, I noticed the sun shining brighter in one patient room than in the rest. It was coming from 406, Steven Waterman's room. Mrs. Waterman, every morning, would open Steven's blinds to welcome the new day. It was a custom that I anticipated. I looked forward to seeing Steven every morning if he was here. Steven had been a regular since he was born. He was the first patient I had after graduating during my residency, and it felt like he was a part of my family.

I knocked on the clear sliding doors leading to his bed. As I slid the door open, I saw a balled-up paper towel flying into the small trash can by the door. "Working on our jump shot, are we?" I asked as the paper towel thumped in the trash can.

"Yeah," Steven said as he balled up another paper towel.

"Yeah, or yes, sir?" Steven's mom said, standing to hug me. "He's been doing this since he woke up. How are you, Dr. Williams?"

"Good," I said, breaking from our daily hug.

Steven tossed another paper towel toward the trash can, its trajectory grazing the rim before slipping in. "What's your percentage?"

He crumpled another paper towel, replying, "60 percent from the field."

"Not too shabby. Sounds like MJ in his prime."

"Who?" he asked, appearing bewildered.

I clasped my face with both hands, exclaiming, "You're joking, right?"

"You're so gullible, Dr. Williams," he chuckled.

I grinned and remarked, "Yeah, I was getting concerned. I need to check on my other patients, but remember, buddy, elbow straight and follow through. I'll swing by later to see how you're doing." Steven returned my smile and effortlessly tossed the paper towel into the trash can again, maintaining eye contact.

"Alright, I got you." I leaned in, and we performed our customary handshake: a high five transitioning into a vertical fist bump, followed by a palm smack and then a brief thumb war. Usually, I'd let Steven win, but today, I felt the need for an early victory. So, when I pinned his thumb, he protested the unfairness of his defeat and accused me of cheating. Laughing, I backed out of the room, mimicking the Jordan shrug. Mrs. Waterman silently mouthed her gratitude to me, tears glistening.

Steven had endured a great deal in his battle with sickle cell disease, yet he never allowed his pain to dim his smile. Witnessing his resilience, along with the unwavering support of his family, filled me with hope for a future illuminated by joy despite life's shadows.

Lost in thought, I returned to my office, my head throbbing with another flashback of my recurring dream, accompanied by a piercing headache. Colliding with my office door, I heard a faint rustling on the other side. Who in the world would be breaking into my office? Flinging the door open, I caught sight of a figure swiveling in my chair, emitting a startled squeak. Before the chair completed its rotation, I glimpsed flowing locks of blonde hair cascading around its frame. Chuckling, I rubbed my fingertips against my eyelids. "Andrea?" I called out, shutting the door.

"You invited me to your office, and then you scared me," she protested, spinning back around. As the chair swiveled to face me once more, it revealed Andrea's nude body. "I tried to surprise you and ended up startling myself."

I stood there, dumbfounded. The sight of Andrea naked in my office felt like one of those surreal moments you secretly hoped for but never honestly expected to experience. All I could manage was to gaze at her plump breasts, sitting gracefully on her chest while her slender waist subtly swayed with each movement. Despite my efforts to appear nonchalant, she looked incredibly enticing in her nudity.

"Are you just going to stand there, or are you going to take a seat?" she prompted, rising from her chair and striding behind it, her breasts bouncing with each step.

"Uh, yeah," I stammered, attempting to suppress a smile that threatened to betray my excitement. I made my way toward my chair, my gaze fixed on her soft blue eyes, which bore an uncanny resemblance to those in my recurring dream. Another flashback hit me, and I saw the nurse informing me that I couldn't visit my grandmother.

Andrea seized my arm and pulled me down into the chair. "I want your full attention," she declared, swiveling me around to face her, bringing me to eye level with her navel. Leaning in, I wrapped my arms around her waist.

"I'm sorry. My mind's all over the place," I confessed, pressing a kiss to her flat belly.

"Well, let me see if I can help you clear it," Andrea murmured, dropping to her knees. She began loosening the straps of my scrub pants.

"You already have, in a way," I replied, tilting my head back.

"Lift your butt," she instructed, tugging down my pants. "How so?" Her hand freed my erection, and she teasingly licked its tip.

"I had this dream, or maybe it was a nightmare, a hallucina tion... I don't know, but you were in it. You were pretty much the only good thing about it," I confessed, releasing a low moan as she took me into her mouth and swirled her tongue around the tip, intensifying my pleasure.

"Shhhhh," she whispered, her ministrations continuing, but my mind remained preoccupied with recent events. Everything felt oddly vivid yet surreal, akin to a lucid dream. I could dismiss it as a typical nightmare, except for the missing memories from Sunday. How did I manage to lose an entire day? Could Simone have tampered with my drink? I don't understand how, when I didn't leave her unattended except when she was in the bathroom. And then she emerged unclothed. None of it made any sense.

"You okay, babe?" Andrea's voice interrupted as she withdrew from her task. "It's not as hard as it usually is."

Knock, knock, knock.

"Damn it, who the hell is that?" I grunted.

"Shit, did you lock the door?" Andrea whispered urgently.

I shook my head and motioned for her to keep quiet. "Yeah!" I called out, my irritation palpable.

"Dr. Williams, it's..." the voice trailed off, "there's an incoming trauma, and you're needed down on the trauma floor?"

I exchanged a wide-eyed glance with Andrea, who had already begun dressing. Catching my stare, she gestured emphatically towards the door, silently urging me to respond.

"Um, yeah, just give me a moment, and I'll be there," I replied hastily.

"Listen," Andrea said, pulling her scrub top over her head, "you go ahead, and I'll catch up after everyone is down in trauma."

I stood, cupping her face in my hands and kissing her forehead. "Thank you. You're the best thing that's happened to me in a long while."

"I guess you can be sweet sometimes," she teased, wrapping her arms around my waist.

I dashed to the door, glancing back to ensure Andrea was out of sight. As I swung it open and hurried out of the ward towards the Emergency steps, the throbbing ache in my head protested against the rapid descent down four flights of stairs. Yet, it was faster than waiting for the elevators. Bursting out of the stairwell onto the 1st-floor landing leading to the ER/Trauma bays, a nurse pushed a bed past the door, narrowly missing me.

"Hey!" I called after him, but he didn't look back. I sprinted to the nurse's station, demanding answers. "What's going on?! A trauma bed nearly flattened me!"

A nurse with long box braids in a ponytail darted between computers. "We have an incoming emergency—a school bus explosion."

At the mention of the school bus, a vivid image flashed in my mind—the burning bus and the children's panicked screams. I wandered past her in a daze, searching for a TV or computer monitor broadcasting news. Spotting a cluster of people around a TV through the double doors leading into the emergency room, I joined them, straining to hear the report.

"As I said earlier, Jim," a male voice narrated over the aerial shot of the bus fire, "as far as we know, a school bus has exploded, heading westbound on Interstate 264. We will stay in the sky as the story develops."

"Okay, Tom," another voice interjected, "we're switching to the ground team. Norfolk Fire Chief is standing by with Marissa. Marissa, can you hear us?"

"Yes, Jim. I'm here with Norfolk Fire Chief Jason Tanner. Chief, could you briefly explain what happened and how many victims there are?"

"Yes, ma'am," Chief Tanner began. "There was an explosion in the bus's engine. We're not sure of the cause. You'd need to consult a medical spokesperson from Saint Paul regarding their injuries. We managed to control the flames, however—"

His voice trailed off as the memory of the screaming children flooded my mind. The piercing, agonizing cries seemed to engulf me. How? How could this be happening? I staggered back from the transfixed audience of staff and patients glued to the broadcast. Pain seared through my head as I pushed my way through the doors leading back to the trauma unit.

"Hey! Are you okay?" Andrea said, gripping both of my shoulders and meeting my gaze.

"No, I just have a slight headache," I replied, straightening up and attempting to conceal my discomfort.

"It looks like more than just a headache," Andrea remarked, wrapping her arm around my waist. "Let's get you seated, and you can tell me what's wrong."

Although Andrea was incredible, I wasn't ready to relinquish my soul to anyone. "It's not that simple," I murmured, guiding her into an empty patient bay and drawing the curtains closed.

"We have a significant influx of patients," I whispered. "I don't have the luxury of focusing on myself right now. Speaking of patients, why are you here? Who's covering the floor?"

"The higher-ups declared it an all-hands-on-deck situation. So, all the attending doctors and nurses rushed down here."

"Wait, who's watching over the patients then?" I asked anxiously.

"Denzel, did you doze off during rounds? The patients are all progressing well with active discharge plans. Except for Steven, he'll be here for a while. Other than that, the residents and med techs can handle any issues that arise. Why are you so out of sorts? This isn't like you."

"I told you I had..."

"Yeah, a weird night," Andrea interjected. "I know it's more than that, but I know how much of a baby you become when the subject gets too real," she said, playfully tickling under my chin. I smiled. Once again, she lifted me up when I felt like my world was crashing.

"Oh," she exclaimed excitedly. "Guess who caught me leaving your office?"

"Oh no," I groaned, hanging my head.

"Yup," she giggled, flicking my nipple. "You should have seen Dr. McAvoy's face. He was very displeased."

Her face lit up with the possibility of getting caught. Even amidst the chaos outside these curtains, with everyone rushing around like mad people, she seemed ready to seize the moment immediately.

"What did you say to him?" I asked nervously. "The last thing I need right now is an HR investigation."

"I told him I was looking for you to give you some message from Steven's mom but didn't see you, so I left the note on your desk. That wasn't the hard part. The hard part was trying not to laugh in his face when I saw him jealous. He tried to flirt with me when he started here," she said, her tone filled with disgust as she slowly walked toward me, a hint of seduction in her movements.

"Uh, Andrea," I said, holding her at arm's length. "I don't think this is the time or place. We can pick this back up when children aren't being burnt." It was the first time I had verbalized it—burning children, the horrors of my dreams, now manifesting in reality.

"Yeah, maybe you're right," she said, looking disappointed. I leaned in to kiss her. She gave me a soft, pouty kiss, then disappeared through the curtains just as quickly as we entered them.

I hung back to have a minute to think. How are there children burning? Does this mean my dreams were premonitions? What is happening to me?

"Listen up!" A southern-accented voice blared from a blow horn. I exited the patient bay just as the commotion started to die and saw the hospital president, Mr. Meyers, standing at the nurse's station holding a blue megaphone. "People, gather around. Before things hit the fan here, I want to reiterate how talented of a medical staff you are. We are about to face one of the hardest challenges in my 34 years at this hospital. So far, we have a confirmed incoming of 16 children with all different severities of injuries. We will start triage in the ER for minor burn patients. Our major burns and emergent respiratory patients will be in the negative pressure trauma bay areas. Everyone else, we will find a place for, and of course," He paused, swallowing hard, "we will take the confirmed dead to the morgue, so there will need to be a team of runners for that as well. You all know what to do. I am confident that all of you will do right by these patients."

The megaphone clicked off, and he set it down on the floor, and everything seemed to return to a frantic normal. I turned my back to the nurse's station and stared at the see-through automatic doors, waiting for the sound of the oncoming sirens. There, I stood alongside a linc of other staff doctors, some of whom I had never met. I scanned the line at the physicians, awaiting the ensuing chaos. White coats hunched over, standing on the balls of their feet, all except one. Dr. McAvoy stood alone, upright. A cold, nervous sweat trickled down his sideburn. I walked over, grabbed him by the shoulders, and shook him.

"Dan, snap out of it. You're an amazing doctor. Probably the smartest guy here. I mean that. I know I give you a hard time, but that's because I respect the doctor you are," I said, patting him on the back. "Let's go save some child's life. Remember, one patient at a time until there are no more."

Dan looked into my eyes, his dull brown gaze meeting mine for strength, and nodded in assurance. We both turned to face the doors as they flew open.

CHAPTER 9

THE BREAKING POINT

I WAS SEATED ON the toilet in a dimly lit private bathroom with my eyes shut. The darkness I saw mirrored the darkness rising within my soul. I felt as though I had tainted the world. The urge to cry welled inside me, but I was too proud to give in. Instead, I punched the wall with my fist and heard footsteps shuffling away from the door.

Knock! Knock!

Damn, did I lock the door? I thought, hearing the handle jiggling. Then, the footsteps receded. I exhaled slowly, trying to regain control and prevent a panic attack. Gathering myself, I stood up, splashed water on my face, and emerged from the bathroom.

I found someone leaning against the wall outside as I opened the door. It was Andrea, her eyes reflecting concern. Her eyes said this was not a vent-to-me expression but gave a "welcome to your intervention" look. We were alone in the hospital's supply section.

"Oh, hey, I didn't know you knew about this bathroom," I said, sounding casual. "Ian, the head of supply, told me about it when I saw his kid for an appendectomy." Andrea stood there, unblinking, unfazed by my awkward attempt at conversation.

"I don't want to talk about it, Andrea," I said, turning my back on her and walking away.

"Denzel. Denzel!" she called after me, her voice growing increasingly urgent until she yelled, "Dr. Williams!" I halted, her tone sounding genuinely concerned.

"I don't know what's happening with you, but we need to talk. You are not yourself. I can see it. We all can see it."

I turned around faster than she expected, causing her to flinch back. "Look, I don't do this whole opening up to people thing. I know what happened wasn't normal—"

"Normal?! You completely snapped and scared the entire unit. I've never seen you react like that over a patient. I'm worried about you," she said, wrapping her index finger around my pinky and inching closer. "I care about you, Denzel, and I want to be here for you if you'd just let me."

I wanted to open up to her. Having someone to confide in again would be comforting. But the more I dwelled on it, the more Gianna's departure weighed on my mind. The look of disgust and hate had haunted me every day since she left. I couldn't risk losing someone again. So, reluctantly, I reassured her I would be okay and left her standing alone in the hallway.

Before my mental breakdown, the trauma doors swung open, and my body went into autopilot. I was in my natural element. It was exhilarating, like a chef in a busy kitchen or a rapper freestyling over a booming track. The doctors filed alongside the incoming stretchers one by one, receiving updates and diving straight into action. Finally, it was Dan and I eagerly waiting our turn. I glanced at bay four and saw Andrea and some other nurses bustling around, checking oxygen levels and setting out copious amounts of gauze and sterile water.

Dan gave my shoulder a reassuring pat. "We're up."

I turned my attention to the incoming patient—a little girl screaming for her mom. Her cries triggered a flashback of the children screaming from the bus window. I shook off the memory and sprinted with Dan to the EMT, who was looking for a drop-off point.

"Hey," I said, "She's going to bay four. What do we have?"

"This is Katie. She's nine years old and was the closest to the explosion to survive," the EMT explained. Dan and I exchanged glances, the word "explosion" hanging heavy between us. Seeing our expressions, the EMT elaborated.

"Someone attached an explosive to the bottom of the school bus. The fire department and police wanted to keep it quiet to control the fear of a terrorist attack. The blast reached back to the fifth row where Katie was sitting. She has burns covering 70 percent of her body and smoke inhalation." Katie's deafening screams echoed down the hall as we rolled her toward bay four. Her cries gradually weakened, and her eyes rolled back into her skull.

"Shit, she's unconscious," I exclaimed as we rolled into the bay. "Okay, let's get her on this bed now! On my count! 1...2. ..3." Dan, Andrea, the EMT, and I transferred Katie from the gurney to the trauma bed. "Katie? Can you hear me?" I said, tapping her unburned shoulder. Katie's eyes fluttered open briefly before shutting again.

"I have a pulse, but it's weak," Andrea reported from across the bed.

"You!" Dan barked at the wide-eyed med tech standing at the foot of the bed. Run and get us a crash cart." Looking all of 19 and likely high, the med tech stared back at Dan with a confused stutter: "Aaa, wh, what?"

"Jesus fucking Christ! What are you, an idiot?" Dan snapped. "The big red box on wheels that has the paddles, you know, the kind that saves lives."

"I'm losing the pulse, beginning CPR," Andrea called out. Katie's burns stretched from her thighs to her chest. We had to be careful but effective. Andrea knelt on the bed over Katie to administer chest compressions while I positioned myself at the top of her head to prepare for intubation.

"Hello?!" Dan exclaimed, flailing his arms at the med-tech, who couldn't tear his gaze away from the dying little girl. "Go already!" The med-tech sprinted out of the room, colliding with the sliding door on his way out.

"You guys got everything from here, right?" The EMT said, backing out of the bay doors, but no one responded. There was no time to waste.

With my laryngoscope in hand, I tilted her head toward me, staring down into her throat, and inserted the dull, sickle-like blade. Before I could ask, Dan handed me a pediatric-size Endotracheal tube to insert. The bay doors slid open, and the crash cart finally arrived, wielded by the still-shaken med-tech.

He rolled the cart to Dan's side and powered up the defibrillator. As I secured my intubation tubing, I looked at the med-tech and asked, "First trauma patient?" He nodded, his gaze fixed on the patient. "Don't feel bad, kid. We've all had our first. Hurry, attach these pads to her, and stand back to watch us."

Two hours passed as we tried to resuscitate Katie. Two hours, and still no pulse. No sign of life, no hope, for everyone except me. Dan stared at me as I frantically performed chest compressions, counting aloud. "15...16...17." I will not give up. I cannot give up. All I could think of was freezing up in my dream and not saving at least one of those kids.

"Hey, Denzel," Dan said, walking around the bed and gently touching my shoulder.

"19...20...21." I continued to count as if he had said nothing.

"Denzel? There is nothing more we can do. She's gone," Dan pleaded with me.

"23...24...25. Get the fuck off of me and get ready to analyze and shock," I yelled, tears streaming down my cheeks, my eyes fixed on Katie's face.

"We've shocked her five times already. There is nothing else to do," he said, frustration creeping into his voice.

"28...29...30. Analyze her," I instructed Andrea, who stood behind me at the defibrillator. "Dr. Williams, I will have to side with Dr. McAvoy. We've done all we can do. It's time to talk to her mom," Andrea said, her voice filled with concern.

I snapped my body up, finally looking at them. "I am not giving up. This little girl didn't deserve to die."

Rage surged through me from a dark place within. Looking at Katie's lifeless body, I remembered how I stood by and watched those kids burn in my dream. The flashback became more vivid than it had been all day. The screams of the burning children grew louder in my ears. I saw Gianna forcing a gun into my face and the flatline from my grandmother's hospital room—all at once. It was overwhelming. I felt like death surrounded me in every form: my mother's death, hallucinating my grandmother's death, the threat of death from Gianna, and now Katie's.

Andrea placed her hand on top of mine, which was still resting on Katie's chest. Before she could say a word, I snatched my hands away. Full of anger, I pushed over the crash cart and the ventilator, letting out the loudest scream I could muster. Dan and Andrea stared at me in shock, too afraid to do or say anything. Tears streamed down my face as I stared back at them.

"Fuck this! If y'all want to talk to the family, you can, but I'm not doing this shit." I grabbed my lab coat, stormed out of the bay doors, and headed toward my private bathroom.

I found isolation from Andrea's empathetic attempts in the stairwell outside the fourth-floor exit door. Leaning against the wall, I tried to calm myself before returning to the ward. But before I could take another deep breath, my pager beeped and vibrated on my hip. I pressed the silence button through my lab coat. "Can I just have one fucking minute to myself?" I muttered under my breath. My pager went off again. Frustrated, I took it off my hip and threw it down the stairs, praying to God that it broke. To my dismay, the pager hit the third step from the top, and I watched as the battery popped out of the back. Unfortunately, the device proved resilient, tumbling down the stairs unharmed. Realizing my overreaction, I retrieved the pager, reinserted its battery, and it went off immediately. I saw the extension to the pediatric ICU and 911 flashing on the lit screen. Horror and worry washed over me as I rushed back to my ward.

As I burst into the ward, silence fell over the room. All eyes turned to me as if I were walking down the aisle of my funeral. Andrea hurried into the ward behind me. I could hear her panted breath as she stopped.

"Could someone tell me what's going on?" I demanded loudly, addressing the room.

"Dr. Williams," a nurse spoke up from behind the nurse's desk, "it's Steven. He went into cardiac arrest while you were in trauma."

"What do you mean, he went into arrest?" I snapped.

"Dr. Williams!" Andrea scolded, slapping me on the back of the shoulder. "We are on the floor. Watch your language."

Her hit only fueled my rage. I shot her an evil look before turning to the nurse. "What happened?" I asked in a softer, more sarcastic tone.

"His liver failed, his body went into shock, and he didn't make it. We didn't catch it in time. We did everything—"

"I'm confused," I interjected. "What do you mean you didn't catch it in time? Wasn't I told this morning that all his labs were good? Golden, if I remember correctly."

"Let's take this to the workroom," Andrea suggested, tugging at my elbow. I twisted my face at her and snatched my arm away.

Resident Daniel stepped forward, facing the crowd that had formed around me. "It was my fault, sir," he admitted, his voice igniting the rage I was trying to extinguish.

"Explain yourself, Daniel," I demanded, my tone sharp and angry.

He admitted, hanging his head in shame, that he had been looking at the lab values from when the patient was discharged last instead of those taken the previous night.

"How is that even possible?" I strode toward him, my frustration palpable. "Either you have an issue with common sense or a sense of time. Tell me this," I grabbed him by his lab coat and slapped him across his cheek. "Now, did you feel that last week or today?" Daniel had no time to recover, let alone answer my question, before my second slap landed. I felt hands tugging me away from him, but the more they pulled on me, the more violent my reality became. My third slap barely connected with his face because of all the tugging, which further fueled my anger. Finally, I broke free from the crowd and landed a solid punch across his jaw.

"Denzel, stop!" Devon yelled, coming up from behind me and slamming me to the ground. "What the hell is wrong with you?"

It was as if his voice pulled me from a trance. I saw Daniel holding his jaw, blood flowing from his lips. The onlooking crowd seemed to disperse as the action died, but I noticed Mrs. Waterman standing in the distance. She held her head down when our eyes met and walked away. It felt like my mom saw the man I had become and gave me up to the world. Devon pulled on my shoulders, forcing me to my feet, and walked me off the ward.

I noticed a large cup of coffee on my desk as we entered my office. "So," Devon said, drawing out the word, "I'm guessing you don't need this cold-ass coffee anymore. I still want my money, though."

I stared at him, my expression serious. "This is not the time for jokes, V."

"Oh, I'm not joking. I want my money back."

"V, I could lose my job, man. I'm not in the mood," I said, flopping in my chair and spinning around. "This is the very last thing I needed. My world is falling apart before my eyes, and I can't stop it."

Devon sat across from me and said, "You still talking about your dream?"

"That, and my mom's death anniversary, the sadistic person who blew up the school bus, everything with Gianna... bro, it's all too much," I admitted, my voice breaking as tears streamed down my face.

No sooner had my tears begun to flow than my office door swung open, revealing the hospital director, Mr. Meyers, standing in the doorway, his face flushed with anger. Devon's head whipped around at the sound of the door opening, and he immediately rose to his feet upon seeing Mr. Meyers.

"Excuse me," Mr. Meyers said, addressing Devon, "may we have the room, please?"

"Uh, yeah," Devon said, standing up and stammering. "Look, Z, Nicole told me to tell you if you don't come to dinner tonight, she's going to kill both of us."

I gave a nervous chuckle. "I'll be there."

Devon walked past Mr. Meyers without saying a word, his eyes fixed on the carpet the whole time.

"Devon, Devon Smith, isn't it?" Mr. Meyers said, turning to Devon before he could escape.

"Yes, sir," Devon replied, sounding like an embarrassed toddler.

"That's all I wanted to know. Good day to you, Mr. Smith," Mr. Meyers said, turning his back to Devon.

And in the most proper voice I'd ever heard Devon speak, he said, "Good day to you too, sir." Then he walked out of my office. But before he entirely disappeared from my view, he shot me a vicious glare as if to say, I better not get fired over you.

"I don't think I've ever heard him talk that white," I chuckled as the door closed. But Mr. Meyers didn't receive my joke as I thought. His face remained stern but expressionless.

"I see we're not on the racial joke level today," I muttered, though loud enough for him to hear. "Have a seat, please, sir," I graciously said as I settled into my chair.

"For some reason, you think you're in a position to make jokes, Mr. Williams," he said, his tone serious. He never called me by my proper name, and instantly, I knew this visit would not end well. He strolled around my desk and up to me. "Stand up," he barked.

"Excuse me?!" I exclaimed, swinging my chair around to face him.

"I said, stand up," Mr. Meyers repeated in a low growl, leaning over me. Sweat beaded on his forehead, and the glare in his eyes told me he was on the edge of losing it.

So, I stood up as fast as I could. Mr. Meyers pointed to the chair across from my desk, the visitor's chair, and the subordinate chair and shouted, "Sit!" Here comes the teaching moment, I thought, as I did as I was told. Mr. Meyers stared at me as I sat down and took my place in my chair. Being sent to the visitor's chair was probably meant to humble me, but it only fueled a fire in my soul.

"What the hell is wrong with you?" he said in a labored breath. I could see his vast belly rising and falling as he struggled to slow his breathing.

"I don't know," I lied.

"Cut the shit, Denzel. I know you. You may have fooled these other people, but I know who you are."

His words rang true. Charles Meyers had come into my life years ago when I was still in college. He'd prowl the campus library, looking for prospective talent for the hospital. Of course, Charles Meyers was breaking university rules by recruiting on campus, but he practically guaranteed you a job if he wanted you.

I met Mr. Meyers during my freshman year as I walked from the parking lot to the public library building on campus. In front of the library was Mr. Meyers, walking inconspicuously toward the library doors. Opposite him, a young mother held hands with her skating toddler, stepping out of the library. The mother, preoccupied with her cell phone, collided with Mr. Meyers, and both fell. The daughter's hand slipped from her mother's, and she rolled down the path, heading toward the street. I could see the panic in the little girl's face as she flailed her arms around for balance. I lunged toward her, but she lost her balance with her skates and fell before I could reach her. I dove for her, narrowly saving her from hitting the pavement. She looked up at me, saw my concerned face, and wailed in fear.

"No, no, no, no, no," I said, imitating Elmo. It's okay." I stood her up and said, "You're not hurt, yay!" I said, flailing my arms in the air. Her face lit up with laughter. "Are you ticklish? I'm ticklish, see." I tickled my belly and released a compelling Elmo-like "Ha ha ha!" The little girl began laughing even harder.

I looked up and saw the mother rushing to her laughing daughter. She hugged me and thanked me profusely as she walked to her car. Mr. Meyers stopped me before I entered the library and asked, "How did you do that? You sounded just like him."

"Oh, the Elmo thing?" I chuckled. "Yeah, I learned to imitate a bunch of characters. Figured it'll help gain favor with pediatric patients."

He stared me in the eyes and asked, "What do you want to be when you grow up?" This was his famous calling card to every student he wanted to recruit.

My jaw dropped, and my eyes widened. "You're, you're him," I stammered, awkwardly pointing at Mr. Meyers with a quivering finger.

"Yes, but people rarely point at me. They typically answer the question. I'll give you one last chance." He stepped closer to me and whispered, "What do you want to be when you grow up?"

I took a deep breath, deciding if I would tell him the truth or some bullshit story. Something said this guy could spot bullshit from a mile away. So, I straightened my posture and said, "I want to work in pediatrics because before my mom died in the army, she would take me to all my doctor's appointments. Every single time, I was terrified, but she would always calm me down and say, 'Denzel, we should never be afraid of the people sent here to help us.' That little tidbit of advice took away all my fear of doctors. And that's what I want when I grow up, to help children in any way I can and make them feel comforted and safe in my care."

I had expected Mr. Meyers to smile, engage in conversation, shed a single dramatic tear, or something. Instead, he plainly asked for my name, turned around, and walked off. Whatever I said must have worked because he randomly called me one day and invited me to a diner for breakfast. Since that initial meeting, we regularly met during my college years to talk, not about future jobs or grades, but in meaningful, genuine conversation. He became the father figure that I never wanted but needed.

Not much has changed since my college days. I am still the sorrowful child across from the forever disappointed father. "What the hell is wrong with you?" He asked again through gritted teeth, "You punched an intern. The wrong intern, I might add. Do you know who his parents are? How could you be so stupid?" Mr. Meyers shook his fist in frustration so hard that his reddened cheeks jiggled. I opened my mouth to speak, and he said, "Shut up. You know nothing. You may think you're big shit because of this hospital and all the women you sleep with, but let me tell you, kid, you're nothing but a pebble-"

"On a rocky beach," I finished his statement. "Look, Mr. Meyers, I know I messed up big. You don't understand. Some stuff has been going on, and I-"

"What stuff is that, Denzel?" Mr. Meyers said reluctantly, probably expecting one of my lousy excuses.

I took a deep breath and poured my heart out. I told him everything about my mother's death anniversary and my dream that felt more like a hallucination. I thought by telling him, I would feel the weight lifted off of me, but the concerned look of Mr. Meyers only made the weight on my shoulders heavier. So here I am, once again, opening up to another person who can only offer sympathy rather than answers.

"I'm sorry, kid. Why didn't you come to me sooner?" Mr. Meyers said, warming up his chilling demeanor. "That's all in the past, and we can do nothing about it. Look, kid, the fact of the matter is, you hit the wrong person. His parents have big ties to the organization that funds this hospital. And guess whose head they're hunting for? This isn't pretty, kid, and you should take this more seriously."

"What do you want me to do? If there is anything I can do."

Mr. Meyers stroked his shaven face and then the back of his neck. "Let me handle this, Denzel. I have a knack for finessing these rich, power-hungry assholes." He leaned back in my chair and mumbled his thoughts to himself. "Okay," he said, jolting straight up into my chair. I could hear the hinges screaming from bearing his weight. "I have the perfect plan. What do all these dirty politicians do for crisis management?" I sat there silently, waiting for the other side of the rhetorical question.

"Hey, numb-nuts." He said, slapping the desk. Answer the damn question. This is your mess."

"Oh, I... uh, they pay people off?" I said hesitantly.

"No, use your brain." Mr. Meyers stood up and sat on the edge of the desk before me. "They get out in front of every scandal. It's impossible to spin a story if there is no story. Now, do exactly what I tell you. When I leave your office, wait about an hour. Then head to the office suites in the admin wing for your," his fingers making air quotes, "weekly therapy session with our employee psychiatrist."

"Our what? Wait, we have an in-house shrink?"

"We do as of last week. He just transferred from somewhere north, Philly, or New York. So he's only temporary until we find a more permanent one. But that is not your concern in the least bit," Mr. Meyers said. "Your concern is to do what I tell you, nothing more, nothing less."

Mr. Meyers walked across the desk, stood me up, gave me an awakening slap across the face, and said, "Now, what are you going to do?"

"I'll see the psychiatrist when you leave my office," I reluctantly mumbled, my face still feeling the imprint of his heavy hand.

"How about you say that more enthusiastically to the guy trying to save your career?"

"You're right. I'm sorry. I feel untethered. It's hard to explain."

"To me, it might be, but kid, when you see this shrink, don't bullshit him. Dig deep and be honest."

I held my head down, and he pulled me in for a hug and whispered in my ear, "Love you, kid."

"I love you too."

Before Mr. Meyers left my door, I turned to him and said, "You're going to have this psychiatrist report to you, aren't you?"

Without turning around, he said, "Like a research paper," and closed my office door.

CHAPTER 10
DR. CONNOR ELLIS

SITTING IN THE SMALL reception room of the therapist's office, I felt more anxious than I had all day. Flashbacks of my dream continued to haunt me, even more so than this morning. I nervously shifted around on a plush green couch, covered with patches of varied materials masking its scattered holes. My body writhed in discomfort from my fear of being pulled back into another flashback. *How the hell am I going to make it through this session?*

My leg bounced restlessly, emitting a squeaky cadence from my shoes. I needed to focus on something, anything. I began to trace the lines on the carpet protruding from under my bouncing foot. The multiple winding tan lines on the olive-green carpet led to the small, quaint desk of a female receptionist sitting across from me, engaged in a phone conversation. She was a younger black woman with a headset resting on her braids. Her head moved side to side, alternating between her dual monitor setup. I glanced around and saw I was the only person in the reception area. I wondered if she was genuinely on the phone or merely playing the part.

I retraced the carpet lines to the wall panel behind the receptionist's desk. They led to the cheapest clock I've ever seen, hanging crookedly above the psychiatrist's door. The clock ticked loudly with each passing second, and I grew restless as time passed.

Sitting there, listening to the old, dusty, crooked clock, I couldn't help but feel like a lab rat waiting for the experiment to begin. I knew it was time to push past my mental limits, but I had no opinion or say in the matter. I knew nothing about this psychiatrist, yet I was supposed to pour my soul out to him. And for what, to save face? The more I reasoned I shouldn't be here, the more Grandma Pearl's wisdom repeated in my head. "God won't always put you where you want to be, but in the place you need to be." Cliché or not, I hated it when she was right. No matter how hard I tried to run from therapy, I guess God fashioned my destination for just that.

"Mr. Williams," the receptionist's monotone voice rang from behind her monitors. "Dr. Ellis will be with you shortly. He's currently in an urgent phone conference. We apologize for the wait."

"Oh, yeah, that's fine. I'm not exactly going anywhere." She continued mumbling on her headset, rendering my disposition to the waiting, even if I had one, meaningless.

I reached for the small wooden table before me and grabbed one of the celebrity gossip magazines. I paid little attention to the lives of celebrities, but diving into someone else's problems might give my brain a break. So, I flipped through cheating scandal after scandal, took a "Which sitcom cast member are you?" quiz, and landed on a full spread of the newest hottest couple in Hollywood.

"Mr. Williams? Dr. Ellis will see you now," the receptionist said again, never lifting her head. I threw down the magazine and stood up, knocking my shin on the table's edge. The receptionist finally looked up at the pop sound and lowered her head without saying a word. Though the pain was manageable, I still limped to his office door. Before reaching for Dr. Ellis's door, I straightened the crooked clock and walked into his office.

When I entered Dr. Ellis's office, I noticed a noticeable change in the décor of the reception area. The reception area looked like it had gone through budget cuts, while his office seemed where all the money went. There was a calming dimness to the lighting, paired with a pungent smell of leather and old books. Dr. Ellis sat behind his mahogany desk, looking up from his notes as I walked in. More than likely, another patient's records because when he looked at me, he messily stuffed the papers in their folder and stood to greet me. Dr. Ellis stood as a tall, older white gentleman with a thin mustache and grey streaks in his brown hair. He said in a proper English accent, "Ah, Mr. Williams, I presume. It is a pleasure to meet you. My name is Dr. Connor Ellis. Do you prefer your surname name?" he asked, extending his hand for a formal greeting.

"Yeah, you too, and Denzel is fine," I said as I shook his hand, still looking around the room. Walking deeper around his double-wide bookcase, I saw various maroon-leathered places to sit. Against the adjacent wall was a chaise lounge, two upright chairs in front of his desk, and one upright chair in front of a shut window on the back wall of his office.

"Oh, please, have a seat anywhere you'd like," he said, acknowledging my wandering eyes. I rolled my eyes at the chaise lounge and settled for one of the plush leather chairs across from his desk. I could feel him staring at me as if picking a comfortable place to sit was some test.

We sat in silence for a few seconds. My eyes, unable to rest on a single thing, bounced from the ferns on both sides of Dr. Ellis' desk to the massive bookshelf to my left to the small betta fish tank sitting beside a wooden penholder on his desk. All the while, Dr. Ellis stared at me with a slight smirk.

"So," I said, drawing out the word, "I don't know how this is supposed to start. And I can't lie, you're doing this whole 'I'm going to stare at you and not blink' thing, and it's creepy." I chuckled.

"Did you adjust the clock?" He asked, still holding his gaze on me.

"What the hell?" I said, alarmed, feeling watched. "Yeah. Do you have a camera out there to watch your patients? Is that how you get your rocks off?"

"I have my methods, and for a good reason," Dr. Ellis said, finally looking away from me.

"You know you sound like every villain from every comic book ever, right?"

He smirked. "I would guess, in some manners, I do."

"Is this a game to you?"

Dr. Ellis stood from his desk and walked past me to the window behind me. "You don't mind if I open this, do you, Denzel? It does get a bit stuffy in this back corner of the hospital."

I watched him struggle with the old wooden window sash, then bend down to fan in some more cooling air to his face. "To answer your question," he stood tall again, "This is not a game, albeit I find that I will thoroughly enjoy this," He said, walking back around my chair. "You see, Denzel, my life's goal is to help the mentally unstable and the most irrational type of thinker. Now, while it is my earnest belief that you are neither, I believe there is a precise reason for you being in my care. Now," he exhaled, sitting back in his chair, "You, yourself, are in a unique position. You, Denzel, have the luxury of my attention with no limitations. I have been instructed to clear my schedule and focus on you. Why do you suppose that is?"

"C'mon Doc. You should know how hospitals gossip. I know you've heard about St. Peter's illegal fight club."

"Hmmm," He said, stroking his clean-shaven chin, "Yes, the infamous incident of the day. Yes, I have heard of these acts of violence, but I must confess to you, Denzel, that acts of violence are a normal occurrence in my profession. As much so as the unfortunate death of minors, I would presume, are part of yours."

"Ah, here we go," I bemoaned under my breath.

"I'm sorry?"

"Every doctor down there was on nerves and emotional with what happened. I get we are professionals, and this is our job. But we're talking about a whack-job that blows up a school bus full of kids."

"Well, I honestly referred to your overall general work as a Pediatric Intensive Care Provider. However, I find it interesting that you focused on the death of the child caused by the attack rather than the child, I was told, in your care the longest. He was your first patient after you graduated. Am I correct?"

I hung my head in shame. I pushed Stephen out of my head so fast already that I felt like I had failed him. "Yeah, that's correct. I'm sorry, I guess I'm still a little off-kilter."

"Please, Denzel, never apologize for your feelings in this office. Emotions are like an ocean's current. We can neither control nor stop them but must let them flow."

"Wonderful line. You get that from a fortune cookie or something?"

He laughed. "No, but I find analogies are the best way for my patients to retain information."

"So, being that I'm your patient now, a patient with no time limit, as you so eloquently stated, is the goal to have me laid out on the couch crying and talking about my mother's death?"

"That is not my goal, but is that something you feel you need to discuss?"

"No, doc, I was just joking."

He took a legal pad from a drawer in his desk and pulled a golden pen from his flat wooden pen stand. "Do you feel you do that often, joking when pressed with tough conversations?"

"No, I just like to joke around."

"Yes, I see. Since we started our session, you have made that your priority. Are you not aware of the reasons you are here?"

"Of course I do. The fight club, remember?"

"Yes, I remember, but that is not why you are here. I'm sorry. I must again confess that I was given a brief insight into your psyche from our beloved Mr. Meyers."

"So why are you bullshitting me?" I stood, irritated by his little game. "I'm not paying for this, but I can't help but feel you started the meter since I walked into the reception. The clock and the information you're hiding all feel like one big mind game."

"I apologize for my tactics, but I informed you I have my methods, and they are for a good reason. But I can see your visible frustrations, so I'll come fully clean so we can understand one another. Mr. Meyers informed me of your mother's passing and your recent dreams, as you would call them."

"I wouldn't know what to call them."

"Well, we will discuss that in grave detail, but for now, I will explain the method to my madness. First, you probably noticed the difference in décor and the unfriendly reception you received from my receptionist versus the somewhat warm and comfortable approach I took."

I nodded my head, enticing him to get the point.

"Well, in my experience, and please forgive me if this is too forward, but patients with suppressed trauma walk into therapy with the mentality to be in control. This way, they can shield themselves from their trauma but make themselves vulnerable enough to impersonate genuine progress. As you can imagine, this makes my job very difficult. My theory is that the need for control is interchangeable with the strength of suppression. So, I intended to put you in an environment where control was beyond your reach so that we make true progress with the time we have."

"So, this is a game?" I asked skeptically.

"No, not a game, Denzel, but a means to an end. Take, for instance, the clock. When I asked you about the clock, it caught you off guard. Truthfully, I set the clock off-center to gauge if your focus coming into our session was on your actions or anything else. I am happy to say that since you walked into the office, your attention has been on everything but."

"Happy? You're happy!? I knew this was all some bullshit game. So, because I didn't come in depressed and sobbing uncontrollably, what does that make me? Huh? What does all this mean?!"

"It means you are ready to be healed." He sat down his pen from scribbling his notes. "If you would have, for instance, come in already reviewing your actions as being outside of your character, then there would be a clear sign to the root of your issue, giving you ample opportunity to formulate your action plan to recover. Thus leaving my help only to be effective on the surface. But since you did not reflect on your actions, I know that there is a deeper side to you that many people aren't keen to see. A deeper hurt that you are afraid to face. And that, my friend, is where the real healing begins. When we strip away all the protective barriers and locate the core issue, that is where we discover the catalyst for change."

I stood up and offered my hand to Dr. Ellis. "Well, I thank you for the opportunity, but being toyed with isn't exactly my cup of tea, as you would say."

"Ah," he smiled. "Cup of tea because I'm British. I have to say that is rather good." He stood to his feet and shook my hand. "Mr. Williams, you are, by all means, allowed to exit this session for any reason, but I have to stress that this session determines your career."

I snatched my hand away and sized the doctor up. "Are you threatening me?"

"Oh, no, not at all. I have no power over administrative positioning, but because of your actions, I am in the position to give my honest recommendation. And I cannot, in good faith, give a positive recommendation for a patient who is unwilling to put in the necessary work towards their overall mental health."

I stared at the door and chewed the inside of my cheek, contemplating if my pride was worth losing my career. I've worked so hard to get where I am now; it would have been for nothing if I walked out the door. I sighed, sat back in the chair in front of him, and said, "OK, Doc, heal me."

"Well, as I am sure you know, it doesn't work that way, but I am glad you decided to stay. So," he clapped his hands," what do you say we delve into these dreams, as you call them? This way, I can see why the child in the accident affected you so much. So, I want you to start at the beginning, and I warn you that I will only interrupt to discuss how you feel. Is that OK with you, Denzel?"

"Yeah, that's fine. Do you mind if I lay down, Doc? My back is a little stiff," I said, pointing my thumb at the lying couch behind me.

"Please, whatever is the most comfortable for you."

I dragged my feet to the couch, not looking forward to reliving the details of my dream again. The more I thought about it, the more flashbacks came. But deep down, I knew this was the only way to understand what had happened to me.

"In my dream, I woke up next to the woman I took home the night before. She was unlike any woman I've met before. But she treated me like I was a one-night stand. I even told her I didn't want to have sex that night. But it was like she made me her primary target, I guess. Look, I'm sorry. I know how dumb this sounds, and everyone I tell it never believes how serious this is. Maybe it all was just a terrible nightmare."

"Or," Dr. Ellis interrupted, "this could all be tied to a particular reason we have yet to discover. Please continue. When did the fear start?"

"Where was I?" I thought. "I took my grandmother to church." I thought about running into Tara, and consequently, the thought of what I did to her came with the memory. I wish I could forget what I did, but I will never bring it up again, definitely not to a therapist. "I guess it started when Gianna didn't arrive at the airport," I said, blocking the thought of Tara out of my mind.

"And Gianna is?" he asked.

"Oh, sorry. Gianna was my fiancé, rather was supposed to be my fiancé."

"Ah, I see. I also see that the subject is still painful for you. Was the breakup recent?" Dr. Ellis said, walking with his notepad to the leather chair under the window and plopping down.

"Well, I guess I missed my cue to tell you to pull up a chair, doc." I chuckled.

"It is still hard to talk about her, no?" he asked, ignoring my deflection.

"She is the bane of my depression." I paused. "Gianna was the first woman I ever really loved. My mom died when I was ten. Pretty sure Mr. Meyers told you that."

Dr. Ellis nodded.

"So, other than Grandma Pearl, she was it."

"Hmmm," Dr. Ellis said, jotting down notes. "If you don't mind, I would like to quickly redirect to explore your feelings toward Gianna."

I sank onto the couch further, letting my feet dangle over the edge. "It was like I knew, you know? As soon as I saw her, I knew she would be my wife. The way she walked, the way she looked at me. She made me better from even the first day."

"That sounds like all was well. So, what went wrong?"

"I messed it up. I don't know what makes a man desire the perfect woman, get her, and still feel like it's not enough. Whatever it was, it made me lose the best thing that ever happened to me."

"And you not finding her in the airport. Was this the first shock of the dream?"

"Yeah," I lied. "After Gianna, then came the bus explosion."

"I thought the bus exploded today?"

"No, it happened in my dream first. It was like a bad omen. I saw the children screaming and burning alive, and I couldn't do anything about it. I just stood there, frozen in shock." A tear fell down my cheek.

"So, is this what triggered you to break down?" He asked, handing me a tissue.

"Yeah, when I saw Katie die, I felt helpless, just like in my dream. I had flashbacks of children screaming in my head as I did my chest compressions on her."

"Flashbacks?" Dr. Ellis inquired.

"Yeah, I've had flashbacks of my dream throughout the day. But they were connected with whatever people or things were in my dream. Almost as if my dream was coming to life like someone was controlling my thoughts."

"Well, I do not believe anyone has the power to control our thoughts except for ourselves. Please continue with your dream. What happened after the accident?"

"Well, after the accident, I rushed to our house. I found Gianna there, but she was different, dark. The type of dark that feels like you're in a horror film, and you feel you're going to die. At one point, I thought I was."

"How so?" Dr. Ellis asked.

"She held a gun to my head and told me how she knew I was cheating on her. When Gi and I were together, she was an Army doctor. When she would go on deployment, I spent all my time in the apartment that she thought I got rid of."

"Denzel, I am sorry to hear about the hurt and turmoil you've been through, but I must know how you and Gianna's relationship ended."

I hesitated, still being sensitive to the subject. "It was the night I was going to propose. We went to the French restaurant on the oceanfront, her favorite place to eat. I reserved a table for us in the middle of the restaurant so everyone could see. I arrived an hour early before the reservation because I was so nervous. So, I just sat there and reviewed my speech over and over."

"Were you nervous that she might say no?"

"No, I was nervous that I might forget my speech. Out of all the things I did, I never thought Gi would say no."

"Why did she? Did she find out about your secret apartment?"

I thought of the hole I had just dug for myself. I have to tell Dr. Ellis about Tara now, but I don't have to tell him everything. "Worse, she found out about a woman I saw named Tara and her pregnancy. It just so happens that Tara was seen in the same army hospital emergency room where Gianna worked. I didn't even know Tara was in the military. I knew nothing about her, to tell you the truth. All I knew was that she claimed she was pregnant, and I was the father. We argued because I told her I was not supporting a kid with someone I barely knew. Plus, I knew if Gianna found out, she would leave me." I paused. "Tara ended up having a miscarriage, and the on-call doctor was Gianna, and Tara named me as the father. It would have gone so smoothly until she opened her mouth for no damn reason."

"Tell me, do you think the fault lies with Tara?"

"No, I know it was my screw-up. But I feel like Tara made my life a living hell because she shouldn't have said anything, but she did." I don't blame her, I thought, not after what I did to her.

"So, what I can gather from what you have said so far is your loss of Gianna haunts you. I would even assume there is a larger sense of regret than you are letting on. Would I be correct?"

"Don't all problems take deeper roots than what you see on the surface?"

"Quite indeed, they do." He smiled. "Now, referring to your dream, does it end with Gianna pointing the gun at your head?"

"No. My grandmother died before I could get to her at the end of the dream."

"So essentially, you are feeling detached from the people you loved and who loved you. All this abandonment must have left you feeling untethered, like there's a void in society?" he asked.

"Yes. That's exactly how I feel. Detached from everyone and everything. The only feeling I have is pain and shame from the hurt I caused."

"Do you think you hurt Katie?"

"No, but I feel like I failed her, just like I did Stephen." I wiped another tear that fell.

"Denzel, you can't save everyone. That's not your job. Your job is to try and do your very best in the best interest of your patient." Dr. Ellis stood up and held his arms out wide, motioning with his hands for a hug. Usually, I would say no or overthink the situation. But for the second time in his care, I put aside my pride and gave in. When I hugged him, he whispered, "I am so sorry for the loss you had as a child and the hurt from Gianna." Then, he pushed me at arm's length, squeezing my shoulders, and said, "Please, join me at my desk if you don't mind."

"I am very pleased with the progress today," Dr. Ellis continued as he directed me back to the first chair I sat in at his desk. "While I feel you are not the enraged animal you displayed today, I still feel you have a long road to travel."

"Thanks, doc, I guess." I chuckled. I felt relieved and less bogged down after letting my inner demons go. Well, not all of them. I was honest with him to a point—some things you have to take to your grave. But I feel better, and isn't that what's most important?

"If you feel comfortable, I would like you to take an assessment." He reached down and pulled a single sheet of paper from a drawer behind his desk. "I want you to take these questions seriously and be honest and open. Everything we do here is for your betterment. I cannot stress that enough."

He slid the sheet of questions in front of me, placed one of his gold pens from his desk holder beside it, and exited the office. The door closed with a resounding echo, leaving me in solitude. Inhaling deeply, I grasped the pen and commenced the assessment.

Upon completing the evaluation, I glanced outside his office and noticed Dr. Ellis perched on the edge of the receptionist's desk. Her headset lay casually on her keyboard as she turned towards him, absently rubbing the inside of his thigh.

The door creaked as I pushed it further, startling them both. She swiftly pivoted back, returning the headset to its place.

"All done there, Denzel?" Dr. Ellis inquired, throat clearing as he straightened his attire.

"Yeah," I replied, sporting a wide grin.

"Please," he gestured towards the receptionist before returning his attention to me, "let's have a look, shall we?"

Returning to my seat across from him in his secluded office, I maintained my grin. Dr. Ellis settled down and began, "I want to apologize. That was completely unprofessional."

"No worries, Doc. I'm relieved you're not the weird 'go-home-to-give-mother-a-bath' type."

A chuckle escaped him as he reviewed my responses. He annotated at the end of my paper, flipped it over, and remarked, "Your answers, although different from what I expected, shed some light nonetheless."

"Hey, Doc, I was honest and forthright."

"Oh, no. I didn't mean that as a criticism. Allow me to elaborate. This assessment was designed to assess for a condition known as Depersonalization Disorder, also called Derealization Disorder." He noticed my puzzled expression.

"Essentially, it entails feeling disconnected from oneself or one's reality, akin to living in a perpetual dream. It's a form of depression. Based on your test scores and our discussion,

I believe you haven't yet developed this condition. However, considering your recent breakup and the suppressed emotions stemming from your mother's passing, I suspect you're on the verge of this diagnosis."

"So, you're suggesting these dreams are driving me insane?"

"Not at all." He leaned forward in his chair. "I believe the human mind can only bear so much pain before it fractures. These dreams, I think, have emerged as a result of your suppressed trauma surrounding your mother's passing and, more recently, Gianna's departure. Dreams can sometimes act as a gateway to the subconscious, and I believe that's precisely what yours is doing—unlocking the memories and emotions you've tried to bury."

"Doc, it's a lot to wrap my head around."

"I understand it's overwhelming, and I don't expect you to process it all in one go. But the most crucial takeaway is that I won't recommend your dismissal to Mr. Meyers."

My face brightened, a glimmer of hope sparking within me. "Thank you, Dr. Ellis. I can't express how relieved I am to hear I'm not losing my job. All I want is to focus on helping my patients and-"

"Mr. Williams, I don't want to give you false hope. While I'm not advocating for your termination, I'm also not yet approving your return to work until you show signs of mental improvement."

"Mental improvement? So, I have to jump through hoops to keep my job?"

"Well, yes, in a sense. You experienced a mental breakdown that resulted in you assaulting a colleague. Consequently, I can't clear you for regular work until we address the pain you're holding onto."

"So, what now? Will I still get paid? I have bills to pay."

"I can't speak to that. That's a matter between you and Mr. Meyers. However, I do have a plan for you to see me three times a week. Don't worry," he reassured, noticing my shock. "The frequency will decrease over time. I want the initial phase to be intensive, almost like aggressive cancer treatment. We need to jolt your mind, allowing you to feel and eventually heal. Then, we'll transition to weekly sessions for maintenance. Does that sound agreeable to you?"

"Do I even have a choice?"

"Denzel, you always have choices in life. You're simply accountable for understanding the consequences and rewards of those choices."

"So, essentially, what you're saying is, I don't have a choice."

"To keep your job, your living situation, and your current way of life? No, you don't really have a choice," Dr. Ellis chuckled. I rose from my seat and extended my hand. He clasped it firmly, his grip stronger than when we first met, and remarked, "I'll see you in a couple of days. Schedule an appointment with Jessica on your way out."

CHAPTER II
A SPIRITUAL CONNECTION

I LEFT DR. ELLIS' office, feeling a strange mix of uncertainty. The mandated session hadn't brought the clarity I hoped for. Truthfully, I wasn't even sure what I was hoping to uncover, but receiving a diagnosis that seemed to scratch only the surface of my experiences left me unsettled. I still couldn't grasp why my dreams felt like a parallel reality and were now seeping into my waking life. Perhaps it was my inability to articulate it. But how do you explain living through your worst nightmares, realizing they were dreams, only to be haunted by flashbacks as if you're still trapped within them?

As I walked down the hall toward the elevators leading to the parking garage connector, I attempted to distract myself from another haunting flashback. My gaze wandered to the plaques adorning what we affectionately called the "hallway of fame." The administrative wing of Saint Joseph's held historical significance, being the original hospital constructed in 1926. It had undergone a rustic transformation into an impressive office wing after the children's hospital expanded into a modern building around 1995. At the entrance to the wing hung portraits of the founders of Saint Joseph, alongside those of esteemed physicians, nurses, and administrative staff who had either retired or passed away, commemorated in the Hallway of Fame.

Taking my time, I studied the smiling faces of those dedicated to their profession. Each individual on the wall had answered the call to serve and solemnly vowed to devote themselves to the company and its patients. Pausing, I focused on the first Black individual depicted on the wall, Mary-Louise Robinson. She had served as a trauma nurse at the hospital from 1941 to 1985. The summary beneath her portrait spoke volumes:

Mary-Louise Robinson was the first Black nurse employed at Saint Joseph's Children's Hospital. Enduring racism and sexism amidst the turmoil of World War II, "Mary-Lou" displayed exceptional resilience. Starting her journey as a trauma nurse, she later pursued a career as a physician and rose to serve on the board of directors for an extensive tenure. Her legacy epitomizes the true essence of service.

"Denzel?" a voice called out from further down the hall.

My head throbbed with pain as I turned toward the voice. I saw Gianna striding towards me with a fierce intensity, mirroring the glare she had when she once held a gun to my head. Instinctively, I wanted to flee, but my feet felt anchored, like I was sunken in cement. All I could do was stand there in shock as she drew nearer. With a smirk, she reached out her hand toward me, and I instinctively slapped it away, bracing myself for a blow to the face.

"What's gotten into you?" A voice, not Gianna's, pierced through the tension. I blinked repeatedly, and Angela stood before me, fists clenched. "I stayed back after my shift just to check up on you, and you swat my hand away like I'm about to attack you."

I remained rooted in place, my feet refusing to budge, as I blinked, half-expecting Gianna to reappear. "I'm sorry. I don't know why I did that," I finally managed to stammer out.

"Don't lie to me, Denzel. You did. I saw the fear in your eyes. You were more than afraid; you were terrified of me."

"Oh, that was nothing. I was just rereading Dr. Robinson's plaque, and you caught me off guard," I offered, forcing a smile to deflect.

"You know, I never realized how much you lie, Denzel. I saw the fear in your eyes, and then you looked at me with a bright smile like everything was fine. You know what..." Angela trailed off, turning abruptly and walking away.

The correct response would have been to chase after her. But what would I even say? Instead, I stood there, watching the last woman who cared for me walk away because of my deceit. What was wrong with me? Why did I always seem to ruin everything I touched?

I continued down the hall toward the elevators, my gaze fixed on the floor, my steps heavy with regret. As I passed the chapel, something inexplicable drew my attention to its open doors. I had never set foot in that chapel in all my years at the hospital, yet now I felt compelled to enter. I crossed the threshold and found myself standing in the atrium, empty except for rows of pews and a faux stained glass portrait of Jesus adorning the wall behind the pulpit.

Approaching the portrait, I recalled the last time I had spoken to God. In front of the portrait stood a clear podium, its surface adorned with an open Bible. Stepping onto the elevated stage, I glanced down and read the highlighted verse.

Create in me a clean heart, O God, and renew a right spirit within me. Cast me not away from thy presence, and take not your Holy Spirit from me Restore unto me the joy of thy salvation, and uphold me with thy free spirit. Then will I teach transgressors thy ways, and all sinners shall be converted unto thee.

"Oh, I'm sorry. I didn't realize you were here," a voice said. "Do you need any help?"

I glanced up to see a younger white man in a plaid shirt and khakis emerging from a room beside the pulpit. "I don't think so. I've just never been in here before," I replied, attempting to avoid further conversation.

The man smiled. "You know, if I had the kind of day you've had, I might find myself here too."

"Do I know you?" I asked, doubling back with a hint of attitude. "You seem to know quite a bit about me."

"Dr. Williams, I'm Chaplain Duncan. We've actually met three times already."

"Oh, I'm sorry. I didn't recognize..."

"You wouldn't remember me if you tried. I don't think I'm quite at the status of being considered your colleague," Chaplain Duncan interjected.

I studied his unassuming demeanor, his multi-shaded plaid shirt, and his worn boat shoes. "Yeah, probably not," I remarked, turning away, regretting my decision to enter the chapel.

"I do, however, know what others have confided in me."

I spun back around, my blood boiling. "What are you trying to say? Just spit it out. Because all the church ever does is point out everyone's flaws. I don't need you to tell me my life is a mess. I already know!" I snapped.

Chaplain Duncan met my gaze calmly. "I've been told that you're a once-in-a-lifetime physician. The kind every man wants to be and every woman wants to be with. Some believe you're on the fast track to the 'hallway of fame.' That's what people who know you have said. But do you know what I see?"

"Why should I care about your opinion of me?" I retorted.

"I see a man who is hurting," he replied, as if my question meant nothing to him. "A man who spends his life helping others, yet struggles to hold himself together. I see that because I've walked in those shoes. So, I'll ask again, do you need any help?"

Chaplain Duncan's words pierced through the barriers I had erected, speaking to my soul like he had known me for years. Uncertain of what to say, I simply nodded in shame. He gestured towards the front pew, and I looked down at his outstretched hand, feeling mentally exhausted at the prospect of opening up to yet another stranger.

"You don't have to sit, but it's more comfortable that way," Chaplain Duncan said, taking a seat. "Tell me what's going on," he added as I reluctantly settled beside him.

"Chaplain Duncan, I've been through this so many times today, and I don't think I can go through it again," I confessed.

"Son, I'm not as concerned with today's actions as I am with who you are. When you look past all your mistakes and trauma, who is the person looking back at you?" he probed.

"I never really thought about it," I admitted.

"Most people don't. A person's past is crucial to who we truly are, yet most spend a lifetime trying to forget," he remarked.

"Sounds like me," I replied, struggling to muster a smile. "But I guess I was blessed. I had my grandmother and didn't end up in a group home."

"That's one way to look at it," Chaplain Duncan agreed.

"Is there another?" I asked.

He rose from his seat and began pacing, his gaze directed upward as if seeking guidance from God. "I want to articulate my thoughts accurately because I need you to hear what I'm saying, not how I'm saying it. You grew up differently but not unlike anyone else," he explained, meeting my gaze. "Oh, don't be offended. You've endured some trauma that most people couldn't handle if they were in your shoes. But what about their trauma? Would a person find it easier or more difficult to deal with their trauma if they swapped lives with someone else? The trauma we face doesn't change who we are. What changes is how we perceive ourselves and the world around us."

I was speechless. I had never delved this deeply into self-reflection. It felt like I had spent most of my life escaping everything. Now, attempting to confront the things I had worked so hard to forget made me feel like a coward.

"I'm observing your expression, Dr. Williams, and I don't want you to feel disheartened. I'm simply suggesting that you must confront yourself honestly. In that honesty lies healing, redemption, and peace."

"So, how do I do that? I mean, you seem to have all the solutions," I asked Chaplain Duncan, my cry for help hidden by sarcasm.

He resumed his seat beside me. "I only have solutions to the problems I've endured. I can't tell you how to confront your truth because you're the only one who knows it. And if we're alike, I'd assume you've buried your truth so deep that only you can access it. It's up to you whether you want to unearth it. But I must warn you, if you embark on this journey, you can't stop and must be brutally honest with yourself. Through that persistence and truth, you'll find healing and your path to peace. I can promise you that." With a pat on my shoulder, Chaplain Duncan rose again. "Now, I'm heading home to my wife, who's probably upset our dinner is getting cold. Take all the time you need."

I watched him stride down the aisle toward the exit, disappearing without a backward glance. Turning to face the stained-glass depiction of Jesus, I contemplated all he had endured. Despite the curses, the spitting, and the beatings, he remained true to himself. How could I emulate that? And what did Chaplain Duncan mean by "path to peace"?

My phone buzzed in my pocket, and I saw Grandma Pearl calling. I hesitated, trying to anticipate the reason for her call, but I couldn't bring myself to answer. Pocketing the phone, I found myself unable to tear my gaze away from Jesus's eyes. Unsure of what I was seeking, I reached out for something intangible.

A few minutes later, I exited the chapel, took the elevator to the second floor, and made my way through the connector to the parking garage when my phone buzzed again. It was Grandma Pearl, and I knew better than to ignore her call twice. That never ended well. Answering, I feigned cheerfulness.

"Hey, Grandma, sorry, my phone was on 'do not disturb.'"

"Why is it I have to hear about what happened to you from Devon and Mr. Meyers before I hear it from my own grandson?" Her tone was stern.

"Honestly, Grandma, I didn't think about it. It's been overwhelming, and..." I trailed off, struggling to articulate my thoughts.

"Don't give me that. You called me this morning, telling me about a bad dream and how you couldn't remember yesterday.

Then I hear about you hitting someone at work after losing some patients. Everyone's saying you don't seem like yourself, and you want to pretend it's all normal. Now, tell me what's going on."

I sank into my car seat, feeling the weight of the day pressing down on me. "Like I said this morning, it's hard to explain. A lot has happened today, and I'm not sure I understand it myself."

"Well, you're going to have to try," her vexed voice turned to anger.

I exhaled, attempting to conjure a reasonable explanation. "Grandma, I really don't know what to tell you," I replied earnestly. "I have more questions than answers myself. I've spoken to a psychologist and a chaplain, and I'm still no closer to understanding what happened to me."

"Mr. Meyers told me about the psychologist, but Denzel, you talked to a pastor?" Grandma's tone held a hint of relief.

"First, I don't appreciate how you said that as if I'm some kind of heathen. Second, yes, I did. He told me I must confront the truth I've been avoiding."

"And what truth is that?" she grunted. I could hear her readjusting herself on the couch. It seemed I wouldn't be getting off the phone with her anytime soon.

"He didn't tell me. He said only I know the truth I've been running from."

"Well, it's pretty obvious it's about your mother. With everything happening around her death anniversary, why wouldn't it be?"

"Grandma Pearl, I don't think it's that. Mom died when I was ten. That was almost 30 years ago. Why would it suddenly bother me now?" Then, I considered how adept I was at burying things.

"Probably because you bury so much hurt that you can't anymore. It's time to stop running, baby."

Her words echoed Chaplain Duncan's advice. "I don't even know where to start," I admitted.

"You start at the beginning, baby. I can help with that. There are some things you don't know about your parents. In fact, I think if your mom had told you the truth, you would have been better off."

"Wait, what? What truth? Like I'm adopted?"

Grandma Pearl chuckled. "Definitely not. You have your mother's face and stubbornness through and through. But she hid some things from you because you were so young."

I waited for her to continue, but Grandma Pearl remained silent. Too afraid to ask again, knowing the people I trusted most had lied to me my whole life, I pondered the potential lies. If I wasn't adopted, then... "What is it?" I blurted out.

"Denzel Eugene Williams, I know you've been through a lot, but yell again, and I'm going to jump through this phone and strangle you."

"I'm sorry, Grandma, but you have to understand where I'm coming from. You've kept a secret from me my whole life, and I deserve to know."

"Yes, you do. I don't know the whole truth, but I can tell you what I know. Your mother was not in the military. I don't know what she did or why she was gone as often as she was, but she was not the military type."

I couldn't believe what she had just told me. My mother's service in the Army was the foundation of my life. So, what did she do if she wasn't in the Army? Why was she always gone for such long periods? It must have been highly secretive if she hadn't even told Grandma Pearl.

"So, what about my dad? If she was never in the military, then what happened to my dad?"

She paused briefly, perhaps regretting telling me the truth, hearing the hurt in my voice. "I'm not sure. I never met him, but I know he was murdered, and it broke your mother. I'd never seen her like that when it happened. She was frantic and paranoid. It was the reason you all moved to Chicago."

"We lived somewhere before Chicago. Where?"

"I don't know. There was a time when I hadn't spoken to your mother for almost a decade. Then she called me one day and said she was in Chicago and needed me to fly up. When I got there, I met you. I think you were two or three at the time."

"Grandma, I need to process this. I didn't... This is all too much."

"I know, baby. I didn't want to tell you, but with everything you were going through and the things that needed to be healed, I felt it was time you knew."

"Look, I'm going to have to call you back. I have to head to V's for dinner. Love you," I said, trying to rush her off the phone.

"I love you too, baby, but listen, Denzel, do not let this make you shut down. Process your feelings and accept how you feel."

I gave her an okay and hung up the phone. In moments like these, when things became too overwhelming, I turned to sleep to refocus. Gently pressing the start button, my car automatically turned on the auxiliary mode so I could check the time. The clock read 6:39 PM. There was not enough time to sleep at the hospital and make it to Devon's before dinner. Begrudgingly, I started my car and headed to Devon's, hoping to at least get a quick nap in front of his house.

CHAPTER 12

A GIFT FROM A FRIEND

AFTER THE DRIVE TO Devon's house, I parked just beyond his driveway and turned the car off. Instinctively, I grasped the handle to get out of the car, but the aftershock of the bombshell Grandma Pearl gave me rang in my head. Instead, I reclined my seat back and set my alarm on my phone for 7:15. Twenty minutes of sleep should give me enough time to shake off my thoughts and have a sensible meal with Devon and Nicole.

As I closed my eyes, a new thought entered my mind. What if I fell asleep and had another dream? With all my flashbacks today, it would make sense if I had one. But the discovery that my grandmother lied to me my whole life overwhelmed my mind with worse thoughts than I was prepared to handle. I rolled the dice and tried to sleep because otherwise, I would bring her lies up at dinner, which would be even worse for me to process. I breathed slowly, sank deeper into my reclined seat, and drifted asleep.

A tap at my window scared me awake. It was Devon. "My dude, what are you doing? We've been waiting for you to come in for like 45 minutes," he said, his voice muffled by my closed window. I jumped up, looked at the alarm, and realized I had set it for 7:15 am.

"Damn!" I said under my breath as I opened the car door. "My bad, V. I was so tired and tried to set the alarm..."

"Man, don't even worry about that," he said, pulling me into a hug. "I saw you pull up and thought you needed a minute. But Nicole made me check on you."

"I'm okay. Really," I said, patting Devon's back, letting him know it was okay to let go of me now.

"Yeah, well, I don't care, that's all, Nicole."

"You're so full of shit," I laughed. "I hope I didn't ruin dinner."

"Hell Nah, you're the reason she's cooking. She sure don't cook for me anymore."

"Yeah, I can only imagine why."

"Shut up," Devon said as we approached his front door.

Nicole was Devon's first and only love since our childhood neighborhood. Nicole, however, only started loving him about three years ago. In high school, she blossomed from the shy freshman to the "it" girl by sophomore year. Until Devon got his braces off, he was the light-skinned shadow of the school.

When Devon swung the front door open, the tantalizing aroma of Nicole's cooking enveloped me. I gently nudged him aside and made a beeline for the kitchen.

"Mmm, Nicole, what's on the menu?" I inquired, poking my head through the doorway to find her tending to the stove.

"You've got this place smelling like a grandmother's kitchen down a country road in Mississippi."

"Z quit playing. You act like I never cooked for you before," Nicole retorted with a quick turn, flashing a warm smile. Besides, I'm just making some smothered pork chops, collard greens, mac and cheese, and maybe some rolls if you're lucky."

"So, all of my favorites. Nicole, you didn't have to go through all this trouble."

"Devon already told me what happened, Z. Besides, with today being the anniversary of your mom's passing, it's the least I could do."

"It means a lot, having you guys as family."

"Alright, Z, enough sentimental chatter before you make me cry in this food."

As the tranquility settled, I felt a sharp smack on the back of my head. Spinning around, ready to retaliate, I was met by Devon's hand offering a rolled blunt, his body concealed in the dining room. He playfully swayed the blunt in the air, crooning, "Smoke me, Z, smoke me."

Turning to Nicole, I quipped, "Nicole, I'm eternally grateful you're repping the dark-skin community 'cause those light skins are weird."

Devon peeked around the corner, interjecting, "You racist, mother..."

Cutting him off, I countered, "How can I be racist when we're both black?"

"Because you're like an internal racist," he insisted.

"Nope, I don't think that's the word you're looking for.'" I joked, chuckling at his confusion. "But please keep trying."

"Whatever the word is, please take this conversation elsewhere so I can finish cooking," Nicole said sternly.

"Alright, Z, let's take this conversation outside," Devon suggested, leading the way to the balcony upstairs. Glancing back towards the kitchen, he hollered, "And my food better taste good, or someone's getting kicked out!"

Nicole's voice carried from the kitchen, "I will cut you."

Chuckling, Devon turned back to me, "Can't wait until we go to bed. I'm already hard."

As we stepped onto the balcony from his bedroom, disgust, and concern clouded my expression. Devon's gaze lingered on the bed. His lips moistened with a flick of his tongue as he passed by.

"What's gotten into you? She just threatened to cut you," I exclaimed.

"Yeah, and I'm hoping she brings the knife to bed. There's something about sex with a threat of death that gets me going," he replied with a smirk.

"There's definitely something off about you," I muttered, sitting on one of the wooden chairs overlooking the backyard.

Devon sparked the blunt, the glow casting shadows on his face as he spoke, "It goes with one of the things I learned from the pastor on Sunday." He paused intermittently to inhale, exhaling a cloud of sweet, pungent smoke as he nudged the blunt toward me.

"The pastor," he continued between coughs, "was preaching about the value of understanding the love in our lives. He said it was a necessary resource like food or water, but often overlooked due to past pain and trauma."

"What's that got to do with wanting Nicole to brandish a knife?" I coughed out the words.

"I understand the language of love she uses," he explained. "When she threatens to cut me, she's presenting herself as strong and expects me to overpower her."

I flicked the ashes off the blunt and handed it back to Devon. "But you've known each other for years. Shouldn't you already understand each other's love languages?"

"It's not that simple," Devon replied. "It's taken time for us to truly accept and appreciate each other's unique expressions of love. It's scary to open your heart to someone, trusting they won't hurt you."

"I know that feeling all too well," I muttered.

"And that's your problem, Z, you're afraid to fully embrace love," Devon continued, passing me the blunt again. "You're seeking security rather than true connection. Love isn't just about finding a partner; that is only the start of the marathon. The race is about building something meaningful together to pass on."

"Damn, V, behind all the Ebonics you use, I sometimes forget how wise you are," I admitted.

"It's not me; it's the pastor," Devon chuckled. "Maybe it's a good thing you missed church; you might not have paid attention."

His words triggered a memory of sitting in church, my mind drifting to thoughts of Simone and our passionate night together. Was there a more profound message I was missing?

"Here, take it," Devon nudged my shoulder, offering me the blunt. I waved it off.

"I'm good."

"What's up, bro? You've got that same blank look you had when I had to pull you off that resident."

"It's my dream. Something you said triggered it, and I've been having flashbacks. The therapist mentioned something about Depersonalization Disorder or something like that."

"Wait, when did you start seeing a therapist?"

I looked at him, surprised that I hadn't mentioned it before. "Oh, when Mr. Meyers dropped by my office. He insisted I go to therapy to save face and help me cope, I guess."

"Ah, I was wondering what went down, but I didn't want to bring it up. Why did he need to confirm my identity, though?"

I chuckled, recalling the earlier encounter in my office. "Oh, Meyers was just messing with you. He's not going to take any action. He only brought you up because I mentioned how close we are."

Devon let out a relieved breath as if a weight had been lifted. "Man, I thought Mr. Roberts had sent him because I've been pushing for better hours. So, what did the therapist say about your dreams?" he asked, taking another drag of the blunt.

"Basically, he thinks my trauma from my mom's death and Gianna leaving me somehow triggered these dreams as a coping mechanism."

"Z, I've known you all your life and never heard of anything like this happening to you or anyone. And why now? Why didn't you start having these dreams right after Gianna left?"

"He compared my brain to a pressure cooker with too much steam."

"Look, I don't want to discredit your therapist, but that sounds like he's trying to pin you with a diagnosis more than anything. Bro, look at me." My gaze had been fixed on the ground, but I lifted my head to meet his eyes.

"There's something off about this. I can feel it. What you've been through is more than just a diagnosis. Did you tell your therapist about spending all day in bed? Or that you can't remember anything from yesterday?"

"I was so focused on why all this was happening. I didn't think of that." I stood up and leaned over the balcony rail, trying to conceal the tears in my eyes. "This situation is overwhelming, V. My mind feels like it's deteriorating. I feel like I'm losing control."

"Look, Z," Devon said, joining me at the railing. "I have a strong feeling this isn't a psychological thing."

Devon's inability to grasp the severity of the situation frustrated me. Like everyone else, he initially offered sympathy upon hearing about my dream, only to assume he had all the answers. I erupted before I could restrain myself, "You have no idea!"

Taken aback, Devon retreated a step and regarded me as if I were a stranger. He let out a scoff before gesturing for me to sit down. "Listen," he began once we were seated, "I won't pretend to understand what you're going through because I don't. All I know is what you've told me and what I've witnessed. You experienced a hallucination that lasted all of Sunday, and then there's your behavior — erratic, unlike you. That points to something more than a simple diagnosis. That's all I meant."

"I'm sorry, V. My thoughts are chaotic. I can't seem to control my emotions. I feel completely scattered."

Devon turned to face me directly. "That's precisely my point. It's not normal. Regardless of what anyone says, you don't just experience something like this out of nowhere. There must be an external factor at play. Nothing else makes sense."

A heavy silence lingered after his words. I didn't want to delve into what he meant or want him to elaborate. I just wanted to evade these issues and never confront them again. Before Devon could continue, Nicole emerged from the patio door. "Food's ready, guys," she announced before we could respond. I glanced at Devon, winked, and silently thanked Nicole for the timely interruption. I rose and swiftly entered the bedroom before Devon could detain me.

"Z!" Devon shouted just as I reached the stairs. I turned around, emitting a noticeable sigh. "Sigh all you want," he continued, jogging up to me. "I wanted to give you this."

He handed me a grey box. Flipping it to the front, I found a smartwatch inside. I smirked at him and remarked, "Aw, you shouldn't have. But, I don't have any shoes to match it." I said with a smile.

"Be serious, Z. I know I'm onto something here. I was going to save this for your birthday, but I think you need it now. I want you to stay safe."

"V, I appreciate the sentiment, but you're going a bit overboard. How is a smartwatch any more useful than my phone?" I chuckled.

Devon rolled his eyes. "Well, I might have tinkered with it a bit." Seeing my puzzled expression, he elaborated, "Initially, I thought of using it as a prank to track your every move, maybe surprise you with a mariachi band on a date or something. But I promise, that's not the plan. I just want you to be safe."

I raised an eyebrow skeptically. "I don't believe you for a second. Not even a little. So, I'll pass." I attempted to return the smartwatch.

He pushed the box back into my chest; the edge digging into my sternum. Then, in a low, earnest tone, he implored, "Promise me you'll keep this on you." I tried to push it back, but he stood firm. "Promise me, Z, please."

Meeting his gaze, I sensed his sincerity. "Fine, fine. I promise if it means that much to you." He hugged me, the box sandwiched between us, pressing harder against my chest. When we parted, he wiped his eyes, cleared his throat, and composed himself. Pausing, he looked at me, still holding the box, and insisted, "That means now, fool." I rolled my eyes and retrieved the watch.

After dinner and a couple of hours reminiscing about our neighborhood days, I headed to my car, the watch Devon gave me weighing on my mind. I didn't want to go back on my word, but I unhooked the watch and stashed it in my armrest. It wasn't that I disliked the gift; I simply didn't appreciate his meddling. Who knows what he had in store with this thing?

Devon lived just nine minutes down the boulevard from me. I halted at a stoplight near the Town Center building as I made my way home. A car sidled up next to mine, pulsating with dance hall music. Glancing over, I spotted Simone's distinctive long dreadlocks.

CHAPTER 13
DESIGNED FATE

I HONKED MY HORN at her when I spotted her. It was rude and maybe a bit creepy, but I couldn't shake the feeling that her pulling up beside me was somehow fate.

"Are you stalking me?" Simone yelled from her car, tossing her dreads to the other side of her head.

"No, it's just a strange coincidence, I swear," I shouted over her music. "But it's a coincidence I'd love to make the most of."

Her face twisted in a mixture of suspicion and discomfort. I could sense her urgency to speed off.

"It's not creepy at all," I hurriedly reassured her. "I'd genuinely enjoy grabbing a drink with you. There's a little dive bar just down the boulevard."

She lowered her head, seemingly checking something, probably her phone.

"Yeah, okay," she yelled back, raising her head with a smile. "I guess I can push my bedtime for you."

Excitement lit up my face. Amidst everything that had happened today, I had forgotten entirely about Simone.

"Follow me," I instructed when the light finally turned green.

As I drove down the boulevard, my eyes darted between the road and Simone's car in my rearview mirror. I silently prayed she wouldn't change her mind and drive off, leaving me alone for the night. The last thing I wanted was to return home and fall asleep within minutes of arriving. I needed a distraction to keep me awake as long as possible. Another flashback of my dream assaulted my mind, this time featuring Simone stretching toward the sky, her dreadlocks cascading down her back. I shook my head to dispel the memory and focused on seizing the opportunity fate had presented me.

A minute later, I pulled into the bar's parking lot, with Simone arriving just seconds behind me. I flipped down my visor and quickly tidied my hair before leaving my car. Hurrying over to her door as she was about to open it, I extended my hand.

"Let me help you out of the car," I offered.

Simone recoiled, her expression filled with unease. "Denzel, this whole meet-up feels... I don't know. I don't want to say creepy, but it does."

I took a step back, understanding her hesitation. "I get it. This might seem weird, and normally, I would've just headed home. But there's something about you that feels different. So let's give this a chance." With that, I closed her car door. "Mind your legs," I cautioned.

"Why are you closing my door?"

"I want you to feel shielded until I've won you over."

She smiled and teased, "Should I start my car for a quick getaway?"

"If that would make you more comfortable," I replied, hoping she wouldn't. To my dismay, Simone started her car with a devilish grin, prompting a smile to spread across my face.

"Okay, let's do this," I said, straightening up. "I know we only met casually. And I'll venture to say you're no stranger to how those encounters usually unfold." I extended my hand, allowing her to agree, but she maintained her grin, shifting her car into reverse and resting her hand on the wheel.

I panicked. "Wait! Please, let me finish. Our, uh, fling, if you will, doesn't accurately reflect what I felt. I felt something genuine. I know it sounds cliché, especially after the fact. But even before we ended up at my place, when we talked that night, it felt like a genuine connection, not just a prelude to... you know." I leaned closer to her car door, locking eyes with her. "Tell me you felt the same. If not, you can head home."

Simone paused, drawing out the suspense. "You're adorable," she finally said, putting her car in park and turning off the engine. "I wasn't planning on leaving. I just wanted to see how hard you'd work."

I smiled, relieved. "Did I work hard enough?"

"We'll see," she replied, opening her door and stepping out. She wore a mustard-colored sundress that accentuated her long, sexy legs, just as I remembered. She glanced at the neon sign of the bar. "Ruby's, huh?" she read aloud skeptically. "So, did you choose this place because it's close or because the drinks are cheap? Because I have to tell you," she said, eyeing the worn wood that housed the bar with distaste, "I don't think I'm going to like it."

I chuckled. "It's close, and I didn't want to risk losing your interest by taking you on a long drive. But I must confess, I may or may not have had a bit of a run-in with the bartender. Just a heads up if he's working tonight."

"What are you getting me into, Denzel?"

"Nothing bad, I promise... I hope. It was a little incident when I was going through a rough patch about a year ago. I might have gotten a little too drunk and could have started a bar fight. I honestly don't remember. Plus, I doubt he's even still here."

I opened the door to the bar, greeted by the faint scent of burnt food and cigarette smoke that tickled my nostrils. Simone followed closely behind, audibly reacting to the smell. Glancing toward the bar, I noticed it was deserted, except for a waitress at the far end, too engrossed in her phone to notice us. With no assistance in sight, we ventured to the bar ourselves. Our shoes stuck to the floor with each step, producing a sound akin to ripping Velcro. I spun one of the empty bar stools around for Simone. "For you, madam."

"Oh, how thoughtful of you to select such a charming stool from among these irresistible options," Simone quipped.

A burly bartender emerged from the kitchen and inquired, "What'll it be?" I looked at Simone, anticipating her order. Instead, she gave me a hesitant glance and requested, "Since it's a Monday night, I'll have a vodka tonic. Extra limes, please." The bartender then turned his attention to me. "I'll have whatever you have on tap," I replied, maintaining eye contact with Simone.

"Why are you staring at me?" she asked.

"Sorry, I can't help it. There's just something about you," I confessed.

"Bullshit," she chuckled.

"Okay, fine, it is. But don't look now; that's the same bartender." It was too late; Simone had already turned to look, catching the bartender's eye. "I told you not to look," I teased, covering my face with my hand.

She giggled. "You know, if you tell someone not to do something, it only makes them want to do it more."

"In that case, don't tell me more about you," I grinned.

"You wouldn't want to know; my life's been pretty dull."

"You don't strike me as boring, but prove me wrong."

She locked eyes with me as if peering into my soul. "How deep do you want to dive down this rabbit hole on a Monday night?"

I gently stroked the back of her hand with my finger. "As far as you'll let me."

The bartender returned with our drinks, placing a coaster on the bar and delicately setting Simone's vodka tonic in front of her. He slid my beer toward me in a frosted mug, causing foam to spill onto my hand when I halted its momentum. He looked at me expectantly, but I opted to raise my drink in acknowledgment instead. The bartender scoffed and retreated through the kitchen doors. Simone reached behind the bar to grab me some napkins.

"You might want to hurry. That bartender doesn't seem like the type to let things slide," I warned, staring at her backside as she leaned over the bar top.

She settled into her seat and replied, "I think I'll be alright. You're the one he seems to have a problem with."

"Good thing I'm not here for him. Now, I believe you were going to share your origin story," I remarked, sipping my beer.

"Alright, you asked for it. So, the first time I catch you nodding off, I'm leaving here with the bartender instead of you."

"Oh, you have my undivided attention," I assured her, leaning my elbow on the bar top with my head resting on my fist.

"My parents were from the island. They migrated here before I was born. Like every other immigrant, they had nothing and built everything they had through hard work. After I was born, however, someone took away everything they had built."

"Customs?" I asked.

She nodded while sipping on her drink. "While they worked, our neighbor across the hall, Mrs. Morrison, would babysit me. One day, my mother came home much earlier than usual in a panic. She rushed through the door and directly to Mrs.

Morrison in the kitchen. She was cooking or cleaning, I can't remember. All I remember is running to the wall leading to the kitchen to eavesdrop. But all I heard was crying and quiet arguing like parents do around their kids. When she returned from the kitchen, I thought I would get a spanking for listening. But when my mother saw me, she cried and hugged me tighter than ever. Next thing I knew, customs agents were barging into the apartment and snatched me away from my mother."

"Oh damn. How old were you?" I asked, placing my hand on hers.

"Six," Simone answered, stirring the ice cubes in her drink with her other hand. "My parents knew they were here illegally. I, of course, didn't know how any of that worked. I later discovered that my mom asked Mrs. Morrison to adopt me when she rushed in. And that's how it was until I went to college. Me and Mrs. Morrison."

"No, Mister, I take it?" I asked, taking another sip of beer.

"What?" Simone looked up from her drink. "Kind of. He died a few years before I moved in, and she never remarried. She used to say, 'People were meant only to be married once. God will only create a single perfect match for you. It's just up to you to find them and hold on until you can't hold on anymore.'" She smiled. "I remember when I was in high school, this older guy in our building would flirt with Mrs. Morrison daily. I would ask her why she didn't talk to him. She would always say, 'cause I'm still holding on, baby'." We both smiled.

"Simone, I'm starting to think you're a liar," I said, meeting her gaze, "or you've just dated a lot of assholes." I continued, "I can't imagine why you'd warn me not to fall asleep. That story makes me want to hold you and protect you from hurt for the rest of your life. Come here." I stood up, gently pulled her in for a hug, and kissed her forehead.

"You're not how I expected you to be," she said softly, avoiding eye contact as I sat back down.

"And how did you expect me to be?"

She paused. "Like all men, nice before sex, but an asshole after. But you seem sweet and genuine."

"That's because I meant what I said the other night. I've changed and am determined to be better," I replied, leaning in for a kiss. When our lips met, it felt like we were the only people in the bar. Of course, in retrospect, we were as far as customers. But this kiss was sensual, passionate, comforting, and lustful. At that moment, I completely forgot about myself, my dream, and my trauma. The only thing that mattered was my future with Simone.

"So, what happened next?" I awkwardly asked, wiping her lipstick from my lips.

"Next? Oh, that's the boring part," she said. "Mrs. Morrison made me take advantage of every opportunity my school had. So, I went to Hampton University and majored in Business Management."

"I knew you were smart," I remarked, spinning my finger at the bartender to signal for another round.

Simone glanced at the very annoyed bartender as he grabbed our empty glasses, then pulled out a pocket mirror to reapply her lipstick. "I can't get drunk," she said as she covered every edge of her lips.

I checked my phone for the time; it was 10:30 pm. "We don't have to, but you did promise to push your bedtime for me."

Simone gazed at me, smiling. "So, what's keeping you up on a Monday night?"

"You are. When I saw you pull up beside me, I knew you were worth missing a few hours of sleep."

She laughed. "You could have just asked for my phone number. You could have also had me meet you at your place. I mean, you live around here, don't you?"

"Ok, two-part question. How did you know where I lived? That's stalker-ish," I chuckled. "And are you inviting me back to my place again?"

"Oh, I'm so glad you put it like that," she said, her voice becoming sterner, my smile fading. "I know the area because I had to catch a cab back to my car downtown. I expected you to drive me, but that option died when you went into a coma."

Her words triggered another flashback of me waking to the sun kissing her face. A tremor of pain hit my head, causing my ears to ring. Struggling not to scream, I put my head in my hands and prayed that the pain would subside.

"Oh, no. I'm sorry," Simone said, rubbing my back. "I was joking. I had figured you were a hard sleeper. Either that or faking. It wouldn't be the first time that either has happened to me."

I lifted my head, grimacing. "No, it's not you. It just seems after my night with you, my life just went to shit."

"Well, Denzel," she said, turning on her stool to face the bar. "You sure know what to say."

My headache started to subside, and I could look at Simone with ease again. "What? No, that wasn't..." I muttered, "I had a horrible dream, I mean. Worse than a nightmare, if that's possible."

"What's worse than a nightmare?"

"I don't know, but I'm living it," I said, staring into her eyes, hoping she would recognize my cry for help.

"What do you mean you're living it? That doesn't make sense."

"Ok, for instance, I've been getting flashbacks of the dream all day. And more often than not, these flashbacks come with a searing pain in my head. I just had another one when you mentioned me sleeping."

"Wait. What? Just now? Are you ok?"

"Yeah," I lied.

"Well, what was the dream about?"

The bartender graced us with his magnificent presence again. He set our drinks down, maintaining his menacing eye contact with me. I returned the stare, determined not to back down. Once he disappeared through the kitchen doors, I turned my attention back to Simone. She had been applying lip gloss. The bottle was blue, but the gloss had a clear sparkling shimmer as she applied it.

"Guys make me sick," she said, recapping her lip gloss. "Everything is about who is the toughest. You all are like dogs marking territory."

"He started staring at me first. I was only defending myself," I said.

"Of course he did," she rolled her eyes. "You sound like a child. Apologize to the man for getting so sloppy drunk and move on." She reached down into her purse again and pulled out a pill bottle. She opened it and poured out an array of pills in her hand: blue, yellow, light green, and a pink pill. A whole rainbow coalition of medicines. Then, she carefully picked up a yellow pill and popped it into her mouth. She looked at me dumbfounded and said, "What?" She reached down, grabbed my beer, and used it to take her pill. "It's melatonin. I told you I have to work in the morning."

"Yeah, well, I'm not looking forward to tomorrow."

Simone grabbed her napkin and covered her mouth. She made a muffled spitting sound and wiped her lips roughly with the ends of the napkin. She looked at me, embarrassed, and said, "I am so sorry you had to see that. The combination of that beer and my lip gloss gave me a disgusting taste in my mouth."

I laughed and said, "That'll teach you not to steal."

"Shut up," she said, hitting me in my chest. "Back to what you were talking about. Why aren't you looking forward to tomorrow?"

I exhaled all my joy as a storm of fear washed over my body again. "Well, I'm not looking forward to falling asleep to see it."

"Oh, that's why you wanted to take advantage of this opportunity. You don't want to fall asleep to have another nightmare. So, what am I, your crutch?"

I thought quickly for a response. "Well, crutches are only given to those who need them. So, I would be honored if you were the one holding me up when I couldn't stand on my own."

"Denzel, Denzel, Denzel. I can see you are picking your words wisely now," she said, sipping her drink. "So, what did you dream about?"

"I'm sorry?"

She smiled. "What did you dream? I want to hear what smooth answer you give this time because you seem to be avoiding the question."

The smile that I had disappeared, and my face felt heavy. "I've been over that too many times today. I just want to forget it. Plus, the last thing I want to be is depressed around you."

"Denzel, you just had to sit and hear my sob story of my deported parents. I doubt a dream could be any more depressing."

"You don't understand. I've had a sad, traumatic upbringing, too, but this dream feels a hundred times worse. Even now, knowing it was a dream, it feels real, like an alternate life. But you were vulnerable with me, so I owe you the same courtesy." I took a huge gulp of my beer and broke down my dream for her from start to finish. The timeline was sporadic as I recalled the events of my dream with everyone else. However, by telling Simone about it, it replayed like a movie. All the while, she sat there, listening to every word. She didn't interrupt me once to ask a question or analyze the meaning of something. She took the story as is. While everyone else I told was shocked with horror, I noticed her giving a slight grin at specific points. I attributed it to her focus going in and out of my story. I wouldn't blame her; my dream wasn't a panty-wetter type of story. When I finished, Simone hugged me, kissed me, and apologized that I had to deal with such horror.

"It was only one dream, though," she tried to reassure me. "It's not like this is reoccurring, is it?"

"No," I said, finishing the last bit of my beer. "But that's the same thing I said to my therapist and best friend, Devon. You remember Devon from the ride home, right?" My voice started to slur and sounded warped.

She nodded, unaware of my current condition. She smiled like she was going to joke about Devon, but her words came out of her mouth just as warped as mine sounded. I shook my head slightly to snap myself out of it, but it only worsened things. My head swam. Trying to hold the bar for balance, I knocked my beer glass down, shattering it beneath our feet. I heard Simone's distorted voice repeat my name, but I couldn't control my body or words to respond.

I saw the bartender come over to check on me. Simone laid my head down on the bar and got up, walking to meet the bartender before he could reach me. Then, trying to remain conscious, I saw his reddened face mouth the word "Out."

Simone helped me up and guided me to the door. She seemed stronger than she looked because my legs moved like cement shoes underwater, yet she had no trouble dragging me through the door. Once we reached my car, Simone propped me against my passenger door with one forearm on my chest, searching my pockets with the other hand. My only guess is she was looking for my keys, unaware of the keyless entry. I tried to tell her, but my mouth had become so numb I couldn't speak. Then, I felt Simone pat the pocket with my phone, pulling it out with my wallet from my back pocket. Oh no, she's going to rob me. In an instant, Simone transformed into a completely different person. All joy left her. I could see nothing but bad intentions in her eyes, and I was powerless to do anything about it.

She tucked my wallet into her teeth and woke up my phone, still propping me up with her forearm. I glanced down at my phone, finding no missed calls, texts, or emails, just my home screen of an old photo of Gianna and I. She walked away, removing her arm from my chest with a blank expression. I collapsed onto the concrete without resistance. My knees buckled, and my head sent my body hurling to the ground. Before my face met the pavement, I wondered if this was how I died. Poisoned and left for dead outside a bar. All I worked for and the good I strived to produce for the world was going with a single thud. My face met the ground, and then there was nothing, just silent darkness.

CHAPTER 14
A FINAL DREAM

BEFORE MY EYES EVEN opened, the clinking of metal and the murmur of multiple voices filled the room. Laughter hung in the air, accompanied by the enticing aroma of brewing coffee and sizzling bacon. All these signals urged me to rise, yet the warm cocoon around my body beckoned me to linger a little longer. As long as my eyes remained closed and I laid still, tranquility enveloped me. That was the plan, at least. But my door swung open just as I reached that blissful state where drowsiness and lethargy intertwined.

"Boy, are you still sleeping?" A voice pierced the room. Struggling to pry my eyes open, I discerned the silhouette of a woman standing in the doorway. The voice seemed familiar yet indistinct. I sat up, rubbing my eyes until they focused, and there she was—my mother. Clad in dark green fatigues trousers, polished black boots, and an olive-green tee-shirt, her hair pulled back tightly into a bun, her face etched with annoyance. My mouth gaped in astonishment as she picked up one of my sneakers and hurled it in my direction. "Get up before I send your father up here to get you," she commanded before turning on her heel and exiting the room, her boots echoing down the stairs.

The words jolted me awake, excitement coursing through my veins. With a swift movement, I tossed aside my comforter and leaped out of bed. Despite my father's recent presence, today felt different—as if I were encountering him anew.

Getting up now felt instinctual; the comfort of my bed had transformed into a reminder of complacency. Hastily, I dressed and dashed to the hall bathroom to brush my teeth. Returning to my room, I glanced at my calendar, sandwiched between posters of Michael Jordan and Magic Johnson. Today's date—June 14th—was circled in bold red. AAU basketball tryouts. My heart fluttered with anticipation; I envisioned myself making the team, executing flawless jump shots that garnered nods of approval from the coaches.

Lost in my reverie, I was jolted back to reality by a familiar voice bellowing, "Denzel, you better be up. Don't make me send your father up there to get you." With a quick gesture, I kissed my fingers and pressed them against the marked date on the calendar, shouting back, "I'm up; be down in a second!"

Walking down the stairs, I spotted my gym bag by the door, evidence of the day's impending tryouts. My father's vibrant and full-of-life voice resonated from the kitchen. My mother's laughter intertwined with my father's voice as I approached the swinging kitchen door. A smile spread across my face; it felt like walking into a sanctuary of love.

Pushing open the door, I beheld him—my tall, slender father, immaculately dressed in a crisp white shirt and long black tie.

His perfectly groomed goatee and radiant smile filled me with warmth. Wrapping his arms around my mother from behind, he rested his head on her shoulder as she prepared breakfast, her playful protestations accompanied by a gentle swat with a floral oven mitt. The shared smile between my parents filled me with a sense of wholeness.

"Stop it, woman. You know I can't control myself when I see you in uniform," he remarked, making his way to the kitchen table. Seated, he gestured for me to join him. "You've got perfect timing, kid. Your mother tried to coerce me into having another baby with her. Can you believe she'd stoop so low? She's trying to break our bond, son."

Leaning against my dad's lap, I shot a playful glance at my mom. "Momma, you're so selfish. I can't believe you'd do something like that."

"What I can't believe is that you believe this crazy man," she retorted, flipping the bacon. "Now, from where I stand, both of you rely on me to cook. So, I'd think twice before pledging your allegiance, Denzel."

Glancing at my father, I quipped, "Sorry, pops, but you're on your own." My parents' laughter erupted.

"Ain't that a shame," my father teased, pushing me away. "A man can't even rely on his one true heir in his own home."

I shrugged as my mom placed a plate of waffles, eggs, and bacon before us. "Hey, momma," I called out, plate in hand, "can I have another waffle? I need the energy."

"Oh, yeah. It's your big tryout today, isn't it?" my dad remarked, focusing on his meal.

I nodded, suddenly feeling a wave of nerves wash over me. Until then, I had been excited about the tryouts, but my dad's mention of them made me anxious. I could sense his disappointment if all those hours of practice amounted to nothing. "You're not coming to the tryouts, are you?"

"And miss my boy shine? Hell, nothing can keep me away," he exclaimed, then quickly added, "I'll put a dollar in the swear jar later, baby," realizing his language.

My mom turned from making my second waffle. "You better," she warned, sliding the waffle onto my plate. "Now, Denzel, why don't you want your father there? You guys spent a lot of time practicing and preparing for this. I'm sure he wants to see you do your best."

"I know." I ambled back to the table. "I'll get too nervous if he's there watching me. It's different playing when no one can see you. I-" my father interjected.

"Son, you don't have to worry. I know how nerve-racking tryouts can be. I don't have to be there to support you. As long as you know, team or no team, you're still my favorite person." My mom circled around him, her hands gliding across his shoulders, before settling at the table. "Just remember what I taught you, son," he continued.

"Fingers spread, elbow tight, and follow through," I completed his sentence. He smiled at me and requested the syrup.

Watching my family eat together felt like heaven. Witnessing my parents' love made me yearn for the woman I would one day marry. Then, the doorbell rang, shattering my moment of bliss. I rose to answer it, but my father held his hand up for me to stay put. "You need to fuel up. I'll get it," he insisted.

Soon after my dad disappeared through the swinging door, Devon's voice echoed through the living room. He burst in seconds later with a boisterous, "Good morning, Mrs. Williams."

"Devon, what have I told you about running through my house?" my mom scolded, pointing a syrup-dripping fork at him.

"Don't trip?" Devon ventured. I laughed, a piece of waffle flying back onto my plate. My father re-entered and playfully smacked Devon on the back of his neck. "Smart mouths don't get fed, Devon," he teased as he resumed his seat. Devon stood awkwardly beside my chair until my mother instructed him to sit down while she fixed him a plate.

My dad pursed his lips. "I don't understand why he eats like he lives here. Don't you have food at home, boy?" My mother swatted him on the head as she handed Devon his plate. Devon and I stifled our laughter, knowing my dad wasn't amused.

"What's up, V? You ready for tryouts?" I addressed him. Devon shrugged nonchalantly.

"Wait, Devon, you're trying out too?" my dad inquired, sipping his coffee. "Since when do you have an athletic bone in your body? I thought your thing was breaking appliances and putting them back together."

"Well, to be honest, Mr. Williams, I know I'm not going to make the team," Devon confessed. "I'm only going so it won't look like Denzel is the worst person there."

My dad chuckled. "That makes sense."

"Where are these tryouts again?" my mom queried. Devon and I exchanged glances. If we mentioned the tryouts were at the rec center, she'd insist we return home immediately for some time-consuming chores.

I stuttered, "Uh, they're at Monroe High School." I nodded at Devon for confirmation, and he vigorously agreed between bites of scrambled eggs and bacon.

My dad fixed his gaze on my mom and remarked, "Hmm. I don't know, Verna. Something smells like a lie." My mother's eyes darted between Devon and me as she echoed, "Yeah, something seems fishy. The high school is two miles away. Why wouldn't they hold the tryouts in the neighborhood rec center?"

Before I could say anything, Devon said, "Ma'am, we're not lying, I promise. The tryouts were at the rec center last year, and some west-side kids got jumped before they made it to the tryouts. So, the high school is supposed to be a neutral zone."

I exchanged a puzzled glance with Devon before turning to my parents, who appeared to buy the explanation. In Chicago, the threat of violence was so pervasive that blaming any inconvenience on a fight or gang activity often sufficed. Don't feel like accompanying your mom to the grocery store? Blame it on gang initiations in the area, and suddenly, the errand was off the table.

"Well, how are you boys getting there?" my mom inquired, her tone a mix of curiosity and concern. I wasn't sure if she was testing us or offering to pick us up.

"The bus," I quickly responded before she could extend an offer.

"Well," my mom interjected between sips of her coffee, "make sure you guys come straight back here after. I have some things I want you to do."

"Uh," Devon faltered, "my grandmother needs me to wash our dog this afternoon for her vet appointment tomorrow."

I gave Devon a warning look and said, "Remember, V, your grandmother told us the vet rescheduled the appointment, so you don't have to wash Sophie." Devon's eyes widened in surprise as I silently conveyed that if I was working, he was too.

"Well, isn't that fortunate?" my mom remarked, smirking with my dad.

I nudged Devon and urged, "V, let's go. I want to get some shots up before anyone else arrives."

Glancing at the stove, Devon checked the time and remarked, "Man, tryouts aren't until 12, and it's only 9:30." Without a word, I cleared our plates, disposed of the leftover food, and deposited the dishes in the sink. "Hey! I was still eating that," Devon protested as I opened the trash can.

I looked back at him and said, "Well, if you want to finish, you can eat them waffles from the trash." His expression twisted with anger, and I couldn't help but laugh. After rinsing the plates in the sink, I turned to hug my dad. "Wish me luck, pop."

My father met my gaze directly and said, "Good luck, son. But regardless of the outcome, I'm already so proud of you." His words felt genuine, and suddenly, the basketball tryouts seemed inconsequential. All that mattered was the pride I felt from my father, my superhero.

Hurrying to kiss my mother before heading out with Devon, I grabbed our gym bags. But before we could reach the front door, my mother's voice halted us. "Stop running in my house!"

The sound of the front door slamming shut felt like a freedom stamp. Devon shot me a look and grumbled, "Really?! You just had to rope me into doing your chores with you. And I'm still steamed about my food."

I met his gaze squarely. "Did you want to stick around longer to showcase how bad you are at lying?" Devon glanced down, shaking his head. "Thought not," I replied, swinging my gym bag from my side to my back.

Devon's ridiculous lie lingered in my mind as we walked to the neighborhood rec center. "I can't believe you resorted to inventing a gang war. You're lucky she didn't go all protective mom on us and drive us there."

Devon leaped off the curb into the street. "It was the first thing that popped into my head. Besides, I didn't see you coming up with any brilliant excuses."

"You didn't give me a chance. You made Chicago sound like Compton before I could even say anything. Anyway, what's the plan after tryouts?"

Devon grinned widely, rubbing his hands together. "I was chatting with Keisha and Nicole, and they invited us over."

"Keisha?" She wasn't exactly my first choice of company. But Nicole, with her movie-star looks, had been Devon's crush since kindergarten. It seemed like a lose-lose situation for me. "Man, I don't know," I hesitated as we neared the rec center parking lot. "Can't we do something else? Go to the mall or anything?"

"I see you're aiming for a lifetime membership in the Virgin Club." Devon's sarcasm was palpable. "First opportunity to lose it, and you're chickening out."

"I'm not chickening out," I retorted. "Keisha's kind of annoying, and you'll be busy with Nicole, so what am I supposed to do?"

"Keisha!" Devon stated it as if it were a simple math problem.

We walked into the rec center, discussing the ins and outs of our plan to lose our virginity. Devon's idea sounded like a low-budget movie. He wanted to walk into their house, have a little conversation, wink, and gesture with his head to Nicole to go upstairs, and she would lead him upstairs.

"Wait," I said, "Is it already planned that we will have sex?"

Devon shook his head, somehow still confident in his plan. I shook my head in disbelief and walked onto the basketball court after we signed in at the front desk. After about an hour of shooting around, players crowded the court. Soon after that, the coach walked in. My nerves got the best of me as he told us to align for what position we wanted to play. I took my place around the middle of the pack, going out for point guard. The entire tryout comprised position-led drills at five baskets in the gymnasium. The drills lasted about an hour, and the coaches eventually led us to a tournament-style five versus five games to 10.

After the tryouts finished and the heavy breathing of 30 kids overlapped each other, the coaches huddled us and encouraged us to never give up on our dreams. It was a beautiful speech, but no one cared. The only thing that mattered was the names he called. Finally, at the end of the speech, the coach called 15 names to hang back before showering. I heard my name called about halfway through the list. I would have cried if it weren't for one kid knocking over a trash can from not making the team. The coach huddled us around and gave us the expectation of being on time for practice and game days and for us to take our sports waivers home for our parents to sign.

Once I got back to the locker room, instead of Devon congratulating me, he looked at me impatiently and said, "Hurry up and shower so we can go." I flipped him off and walked into the communal showers. As I washed my body, I contemplated losing my virginity. What was it going to feel like? What if I don't put it where it's supposed to go? I looked down at my manhood getting splashed with water. Am I big enough? As more questions flooded my mind, I was becoming unsure I was ready to lose my virginity. But I didn't want to be the last guy at school who did. I especially did not want my first to be with Keisha Cunningham. She wasn't ugly, but I was not attracted to her enough to make her my first. But Devon is my best friend, and we've done everything together. I felt like I owed him. I figured it would be better to focus on the act of losing my virginity rather than on whom I was losing it with.

After my shower, I changed into my street clothes and headed to Keisha and Nicole's house. Fortunately, they lived just a street from mine, and their parents tended to work long shifts during the summer. So, everything seemed to fall into place until we heard a voice piercing the air, "Devon! Devon! Boy, I know you hear me!"

We turned to see Devon's grandmother, adorned with a bonnet on her head, clad in a pastel nightgown and worn-down pink fuzzy slippers, pulling a rolling basket of groceries. In our direct line of vision, there was no escaping or ignoring her. Fear rooted us to the spot as she approached.

"When I call you, you better answer me, boy," she scolded, slapping Devon's face. Neither Devon nor I knew how to react. I could only watch in apprehension as she turned her attention to him, her hand connecting with his cheek.

"Help me put these groceries away," she demanded, her tone still laced with irritation. Devon looked to me for the same assistance he had provided my parents before we left for the tryouts. Thinking fast, I interjected, "Excuse me, Mrs. Smith." Her gaze snapped to me as if it weren't my place to speak. "I just made the basketball team, and Devon and I planned to hang out with the team at the mall."

Mrs. Smith placed her hands on her hips, rolling her neck before responding, "Devon ain't going nowhere until he helps me put these groceries away."

"Of course, Ma'am. I wouldn't dream of asking V to skip out on his chores. I was just wondering if he could join us after he helps," I replied, avoiding her gaze and nervously twisting my shirt between my fingers.

Mrs. Smith scrutinized me momentarily, assessing my sincerity, before grudgingly conceding, "I suppose." I smiled, thanked her, and instructed Devon to meet me on Nicole's porch. As Devon and his grandmother turned to head home, he shot me a pained look, and all I could do was shrug. I turned on my heel and sprinted to Nicole's house, praying my parents hadn't spotted Devon and his grandmother.

Once I reached Nicole's house, cutting between the alleyway and jumping a fence, I saw her sitting on her steps, watching Keisha dribbling a basketball. As I approached their home, the basketball hit Keisha's ankle and rolled into the street. I ran after it, catching it before it went to the other side of the road. I bounced it off the curb, grabbed it, and dribbled it between my legs, back to the other side of the street, then passed it behind my back to Keisha.

"Denzel, why are you trying to show off?" Keisha said, snatching the ball out of the air.

"Because I made the basketball team," I said, gesturing for her to pass the ball to me.

"Denzel, did you say you made the team?" Nicole said, jumping off the porch. "Can I come to watch you play?"

Keisha passed the ball to me and stormed into the house, not saying a single word. "What's wrong with her?" I asked as I began dribbling.

"Keisha's been jealous ever since she found out I liked you." Nicole walked closer to me, biting her lip.

Her words confused me. How could she like me when the whole reason I came was so Devon could be with her? "What do you mean?" I coughed, trying to clear my voice. "Devon is-"

"Devon said he was bringing you, Denzel. That's the only reason I said yes," Nicole said, walking closer. Her puberty kicked in last summer, so her chest grew into a full bosom. She pushed that bosom against my chest, giving me an enthusiastic hug, and whispered, "Congratulations on making the basketball team. I want to give you something to remember me when you see me watching you in the stands."

My teenage wild and uncontrollable bulge protruded in my shorts as I could feel her warm breath coaxing my ear. My thoughts raced with everything I wanted to do to her and the hopes of what she would do to me. But the words seemed to be stuck in my throat. Finally, I could only muster a solemn "Okay." The word escaping my mouth was quiet and very unsure, but it was more than enough for a confirmation for Nicole. She grabbed my hand and pulled me up her front stairs. The basketball fell out of my hands and rolled back into the street. She burst through the front door, jerking me inside, and slammed the door behind me. The moment I was in the foyer of her house, I saw Keisha looking at the TV with her headphones on her head in the living room ahead. Within a second of the image, Nicole grabbed my arm and yanked me up the stairs to my left.

"Nicole, Devon is on his way here. He just had to help his grandmother," I tried to explain as she led me to her bedroom at the top of the stairs. "I just don't feel right about this."

Nicole stopped in front of her door and released my hand. Her face seemed less bubbly than usual. "Do you not like me, Denzel?" she asked, her tone almost whiny.

I didn't want to betray Devon's trust, but Nicole was the cutest girl in the neighborhood. Everyone talked about her. And it wasn't like Devon and Nicole were together. "No, it's not like that. I like you," I admitted. Then, without another word, Nicole gave me a devilish grin and pulled me into her bedroom, locking the door behind us.

Her bedroom looked like a pink cotton candy explosion. Everything was pink, from her bed to her fluffy pillows to the pink and white clouds artistically painted on the ceiling. Finally, Nicole turned me around and pushed me onto her bed. Unsure of what to do, I lay back and watched her.

She walked toward me seductively, each step a tantalizing sway. I tried to urge her to hurry, but she silenced me with a finger to my lips. Her other hand grazed over my bulge, and she let out a little squeal, seemingly impressed with her inspection. Standing up, she undressed, unhooking her bra and pulling off her T-shirt.

Nicole then bent down and removed my shorts, my underwear coming with them. She took hold of my erection and took me into her mouth. I felt her warm tongue swirling around my tip. A small but deep moan escaped me, and she withdrew me from her mouth with a loud, suction-like pop.

"Not yet," she whispered. "I know you're a virgin. Devon already told me. And I want you to lose your virginity with me." Nicole stood up, pulling down her white jean shorts. She had no underwear on, which made me nearly explode with desire. Climbing on top of me, she guided me inside her. Her warmth enveloped me, sending electric pulses through my whole body. As she rode me, a surge of pleasure grew in my loins. An electric fire began to travel up my penis, too powerful to resist. Before I could utter a word, my body was numb with pleasure. It felt like I had poured a part of my soul into her. For a fleeting moment, my entire being was engulfed in euphoric bliss. Is this what sex feels like? Nicole then dismounted, backing away with a grin.

"Well, that didn't take long," she remarked, leaning over to kiss me. At that moment, I felt like I was in love. As we kissed, I imagined our future children playing in our yard and our nightly lovemaking sessions.

But as we began to get dressed, the euphoric daydream faded. We heard the door handle jiggling. Panic flooded us both. My immediate thought was of her parents catching us, me with my pants literally around my ankles. The door swung open, revealing Keisha holding a butter knife, saying, "See, I told you."

From my vantage point behind the bedroom door, I saw Nicole's panicked face transform into an evil smirk. I couldn't discern if she was plotting some revenge on Keisha or if this had been her plan all along. Footsteps echoed on the hardwood floor, slowly ascending the stairs, inching closer to the door, and eventually revealing Devon, his mouth gaping in shock as he saw me. With her task complete, Keisha replaced her headphones and skipped back downstairs.

"Bro, tell me you didn't do what I think you did." Devon's voice was low and angry. I tried to explain what happened, but Nicole spoke first.

"Devon, what are you doing here? Denzel said you weren't coming."

"Oh, he did?" Devon's eyes bore into mine. Shocked by her audacity, I had no time to defend myself before she continued.

"He told me you weren't coming. He said that he talked you out of coming so he could get with me. I'm sorry, I didn't know he would lie like that. I feel so bad now." Nicole slumped back and sobbed in her desk chair.

"She is lying!" I protested, pulling up my shorts. "I told her you were coming, and she said she didn't like you."

"So, because she didn't like me, you had sex with her?"

Devon was right. I had no comeback. I should have just said no. Nicole halted her tears, which only she and I knew were fake, and said, "Denzel, you need to go. I can't believe you would manipulate me like that."

Everything inside me wanted to scream and get Devon on my side, but I could see the hate in his eyes as he stared at me. I knew nothing I said would help. I dropped my head and walked out of Nicole's room.

No sooner had I reached the doorway than I felt knuckles collide with my jaw. It knocked me back a few steps deeper into Nicole's room. Before I could fully assess the damage he had done, Devon unleashed a barrage of more punches at me. I curled in a ball, trying to shield myself from his anger.

I could hear Nicole screaming, "Devon, stop! He's not worth it." Eventually, Devon ceased. My body still curled up, I felt my face started to swell. I was hesitant, fearing it might be a ruse for him to land another clean shot. I peeked through my folded arms and saw Nicole had pulled Devon off me.

"Denzel, get the fuck out before he kills you!" She yelled at my frozen, fetal-positioned body. I jumped to my feet and bolted out of her room, my eyes solely focused on the stairs. If I could reach the stairs and to the front door, I'd be safe at home. So, just as I planned, I hit the stairs in full stride. My sneakers thumped and squeaked on the stairs. I leaped over the last three or four steps and landed heavily at the bottom, the weight of my jump getting the better of me, causing me to slide into the front door.

"Denzel!" I turned over, and Devon stood in the middle of the stairs, his face still contorted with anger. He never called me Denzel. It was always Z. "I fucking hate you. If I see you again, I swear I will kill you. That's a promise."

I got up and flung the door open. But before I left the house, I saw Keisha standing in the living room, out of sight from everyone upstairs, with a look of regret. I shook my head at her, turned towards the door, and ran home as fast as I could.

Panting, trying to catch my breath, I stood on my porch, too scared to turn around to see if Devon was chasing me. Finally, I swallowed my fear and turned around. I only saw the quiet neighborhood, still waiting for the humidity to die before emerging from their houses. It wasn't until then that I realized how badly my face stung. A trickle of blood wet my taste buds, and I could taste my pain. I leaned over our front porch banister and spat the blood onto our front lawn. The more my face pulsed with agony, the more I wanted to be comforted by my mother and advised by my father. I turned around and headed to my house. I shut the front door and heard a thud coming from the kitchen. Assuming my parents were acting like their usual selves, being goofy and overly affectionate, I went in to investigate. I could use a good laugh from my family to pick me up.

I pushed on the swinging door and saw my father standing with a look of surprise at my emergence. My father was still dressed for work, wearing his white dress shirt and black tie. But now, blood stained his shirt. He gripped a chef's knife in his hand, dripping with the same. What the hell was going on? I no longer thought of my being beaten down by Devon. Instead, my thoughts focused on the demonic look in my father's eyes. I panned my eyes down to see the blood dripping from the knife onto my mother's lifeless face. She lay there, her head towards the swinging door, her arms flailed to either side, her eyes opened with a dead gaze. A pool of blood had started seeping out from under her body, and I felt my skin grow cold.

"Come here, son," my dad said, gesturing with the knife and wiping the blood off his mouth with his other hand. The blood from the waving knife splattered on the walls and the floor. I just stood there, unable to take my attention off my mother's stiff body. What had happened? Why had he killed her? More importantly, what was he going to do to me?

"Boy!" my dad yelled, drawing my focus back to him. "I said, come here." His voice was low and treacherous. I backed up through the kitchen door and left it swinging, showing me quick flashes of my mother's body on the floor. I kept backing until my back hit the wall beside the front door. I knew I should leave and call the police.

Before I could think to move, my dad exploded through the door with the same rage I saw in Devon's eyes. He didn't say a word. He just stood there watching me, slowly rotating the knife. I went to reach for the door, and he hurled the knife at me, just missing my head and sticking into the wall with a thunk. I looked at the impaled knife in the wall, wiggling.

"You're not leaving this house alive, son. Your mother needs you. You have to be with her. She needs you." His voice carried distinct tones as if he were possessed. I needed to think quickly, or I'd die alongside my mother.

I remembered my surroundings like a light switch flicking on in my head. To my left stood an end table with a lamp, housing a drawer containing my mother's service weapon, kept there as an added safety precaution. Perhaps that was why she had been glancing toward the living room—trying to reach the gun. Or maybe she was afraid I would return to see the evilness that possessed my father.

As my dad stepped toward me, I yanked open the drawer. "Stay back, or I'll shoot," I said, seizing the gun and aiming its barrel at his head. My hands trembled so much it felt as though the weapon might slip from my grasp.

He grinned at me like a sinister cat. "Oh, what's wrong, son? Didn't you make the team? Or are you upset Devon beat the crap out of you?" he taunted, his grin twisted with malice.

"How did you know about that?" I asked, my hand still shaking under the weight of the gun and the burden of saving my life. Then, without warning, my dad lunged toward me. I closed my eyes and pulled the trigger.

After the loud pop, I was too terrified to open my eyes to face the consequences of my life-or-death gamble. All I could feel was a high-pitched ringing in my ears. I didn't know if I was alive or dead. After a few moments, the ringing subsided, and I heard a gurgling sound. Slowly, I opened my eyes and saw my father clutching his neck, blood gushing between his fingers. I realized I had shot him in the throat, not the head.

I stood there, staring down at him, shell-shocked. Eventually, I approached him and watched as he lost his struggle for life. He tried to say something, but it sounded like a choked whisper. "Why?" he struggled to articulate. "Why?"

Seconds later, he lay just as still and lifeless as my mother in the kitchen. Tears burned in my eyes as I reflected on the horrors of the day. I had begun with a loving, happy family and ended up alone, with no hope of redemption. I stared at the gun, contemplating every person who had abandoned me. What was the point of carrying on? What was the point of trying to build a new life when all I could think about was the old one?

Finally, I pressed the gun barrel against my temple—the heat from its recent discharge sizzled against my skin. I closed my eyes, sank to my knees, and pulled the trigger.

CHAPTER 15
DARKNESS

THE SOUND OF THE gunshot jolted me awake. I tried to open my mouth to breathe, but it remained immobile. Instinctively, I drew deep breaths through my nose, then in rapid succession. Why can't I open my mouth? Panic surged within me as I struggled to pry open my eyes, yet they remained stubbornly shut. I attempted to flail my body around, but every muscle seemed frozen.

I've experienced this sensation before, waking up unable to move as a child. Grandma Pearl would always attribute it to a spiritual battle between a demon and my spirit for control over my soul. I would envision the struggle, willing my spirit to triumph, and invariably, I'd awaken victorious. But this time feels different, as though the demon has already emerged victorious.

Taking deep breaths to steady myself, I attempted to lift my head, but still, I couldn't move. Then, a hot, prickling sensation began in my stomach, spreading throughout my body. It extended to my limbs, and though I could feel them, I remained powerless to move them. However, I sensed my body swaying. How is my body swaying? More importantly, where is it swaying?

The paralyzing grip loosened as the numbness transitioned to a prickling sensation and reached my fingertips. I concentrated on lifting an index finger, and gradually, I could flex it. Soon, mobility returned to my other fingers and down my arm. Yet, I discovered both my wrists were bound, and when I attempted to move my legs, I realized they were bound, too.

My eyelids convulsed as I strained to open them, and after summoning considerable strength, my sight returned. I beheld the glimmer of candlelight flickering in the darkness of the room. Three thick white candles stood before me, one to my left, one to my right, and one directly in front. All burned at the same height atop tall black stands, wax cascading down their sides. Their illumination barely penetrated beyond a small radius around me, leaving the rest of the room shrouded in darkness—a menacing abyss that demanded attention.

Examining the ropes binding my limbs, I realized I was suspended in the center of a large metal rack, with ropes extending to each corner. I followed the lines from my wrists upward into the dark void, but their endpoints remained obscured. I attempted to wriggle free, but the ropes held firm.

What happened to me? What's the last thing I remember before the dream? Simone—I was with her. She drugged me, that bitch. I glanced down at my naked body, searching for marks or scars. Fear escalated to panic, my heart pounding so fiercely I felt its pulse throughout my body.

The sound of heels clicking on the ground reverberated from the darkness. Initially faint and distant, they grew steadily louder and nearer. I allowed my body to go limp, presuming my captor would assume I remained unconscious. The clicking ceased, leaving the air charged with the echo of fading footsteps, causing my breath to stutter.

"Do you know the best thing about darkness?" a woman's voice pierced the silence from the shadows. Her Russian accent lacked sympathy. "Raise your head. I know you're awake."

Feeling exposed, I complied, peering into the darkness. Though I saw nothing, heard nothing, I knew she was there.

"Answer question! What is best thing about darkness?" Her irritation mounted, but I couldn't muster the courage to respond. My lips trembled, rendering me speechless. All I could think was that this was the night I would die. The only uncertainty was how long it would take.

Tears streamed down my face as I cried out, "Please don't hurt me. I'll give you anything you—" Before I could finish, a black whip shot out from the darkness, popping inches from my face. I felt the vibrating pressure graze my cheek, the pop echoing metallically, like a knife slicing through the air before vanishing back into the shadows. I writhed in my roped restraints, emitting a frantic yell.

"I warn you, Denzel, I have very little patience. If you cannot entertain me, then I will entertain myself," the concealed voice declared, extinguishing the flame of the middle candle with a flick of her whip. The flame died with the same metallic sound. "What is the best thing about darkness?" Her irritation was palpable and deliberate this time.

My mind scrambled to focus, desperate to provide an answer. "I... I don't know," I stammered. There was a moment of silence, and then the rhythmic tap of her heels resumed, circling around me. Struggling, I twisted my head to glimpse my captor beyond the darkness, but all I saw was the looming void and the echo of her heels pacing around me.

"The best thing about darkness is perception. When you use light to banish darkness, your perception is dictated by what the light reveals. Your eyes are trained to see only what the light illuminates first. But in darkness, perception shifts. You embrace it and recognize the disadvantages of those who rely on light. Do you agree?"

Nervously, I responded, "I suppose that makes sense. I mean, I can't see you right now, but it's obvious that you can see me."

She offered no reply. Her heels retreated behind me again, their approach audible before fading into silence. The quiet stretched on, fueling my panic. My heart raced, and sweat trickled down my back. I tried to focus on the two flickering candles before me, wishing desperately to be anywhere but here. Suddenly, a warm, moist breath pulsed against my ear. Reflex urged me to turn my head, but she vanished into the darkness before I could.

"You are correct, my dear. I can see you and everything you cannot. Once you embrace the darkness, everything within reach is yours for the taking. Is that you? Have you embraced darkness?"

I frantically scanned the room, trying to catch a glimpse of her. Then, a small-framed woman stepped out from between the two candles. She was clad head to toe in a black latex suit. The only visible part of her skin was around her eyes, peeking through the holes in her mask. Despite that, her skin matched the same shade as her suit. I could see her adjusting the strings on the back of her mask. Her feet had slipped from her heels, and she wore black socks. She sashayed towards me, quiet as a cat. It made me more nervous that I could finally see her but still not hear her unless she wanted to.

"I have no darkness to embrace," I tried to reason with her. "As a matter of fact, I have spent most of my whole life running from my darkness. I hate the darkness inside of me."

"You have darkness in you. You use your darkness to harm. This is why I am here."

"To find my darkness?" I looked around at the contraption built for me. "Or to punish me for it?"

"You are smart," she said as she approached my body and mounted me, still strapped in mid-air. Her weight was light, but my body still swayed from her impact. She wrapped her legs around my waist and grasped the rope that tied my wrist. She leaned in close, her masked face inches from mine, then kissed me passionately through her mask. After the kiss, she stroked my face with her hand. "What did you dream about?" Her voice was becoming sweet, almost seductive.

"Dream? What dream?" I asked.

"Do not play coy with me, Denzel. You have two dreams that I am incredibly interested in." My eyes widened in surprise. How could she have known I've had two dreams? The second one just happened. "How did you know I had two?" I thought about my first dream. "How do you know about the first dream? Wait, Simone? You have to be Simone. Because the only woman I told my first dream to was you. But how do you know about the second dream?"

The masked woman climbed down off of me and walked toward the candles. The first thing I noticed was the whip hooked on her hip. Then I saw the sheath holding a dark-handled blade strapped to her back. Her hands grazed the top of her head, and she slid them down to her neck. The rubbing sound filled me with fear, but she seemed to relish it. Her fingers traveled to the blade's hilt and softly stroked the tip. I looked at the blade and then down at my exposed form. The symbolism in this game she's playing will not end well for me.

"I told you, Denzel, I see more than what the light exposes to you. The only thing I cannot see is your dreams. But if you do not want to answer me, I will expedite our night."

She unsheathed her sword, twirling it around her head, and thrust it toward me, the blade stopping an inch from my eye.

I could see the sharp tip held steady horizontally frozen in mid-air. She turned the blade vertically and sliced open my skin from under my eye down to my chin. She pulled the sword back and flung the residual blood off it, splattering the candles and the floor. "You choose," she said, her voice almost disappointed.

Too petrified to scream out, I hung there, shivering in fear. "Okay, okay. I'll tell you."

She sheathed her sword, disappeared into the darkness, and reappeared, dragging a rolling chair behind her. She sat down in front of me and waited for me to start.

"Why are you doing this to me?" I asked frantically.

She reached her hand under the seat of the rolling chair and, with the slightest of ease, flung something sharp at me, just missing my face. It was too fast to see, but I could hear it cutting the air as it flew past my head. She didn't seem the type to miss or play around. That was a warning shot.

"Okay!" I said, eager to stay alive. "I dreamed I was a little kid in Chicago. My father was there, and in the beginning, it felt good. I felt complete, I guess. Later on, I had basketball tryouts, and I made the team. Everything seemed great until after I lost my virginity to my best friend's crush. He burst into the room and damn near killed me. So, I ran back home to find that my dad had stabbed my mother to death." Tears rolled down my face as if this dream were a memory more than fiction. "He came after me to kill me as well, and I had to shoot him," I said, sniffling heavily. "I wanted to run but was so scared, I just reacted. I stood there after, so broken that I turned the gun to my temple and pulled the trigger. Then I woke up here after the gunshot. Now, why are you doing this, Simone?!" My voice crescendo into a yell, an instant regret.

She stood and unhooked her whip that was looped on itself, hanging from her hip. She unraveled it and flung its end toward me. I could see in the light from the flickering candles a metal tip attached to the tail of the whip flying toward me. The bladed tail of the whip punctured the skin on my chest around my nipple. I saw it slicing my nipple from my body as she drew the whip back. The agony of pain was too great to keep quiet. I screamed aloud, too loud for what happened. I needed someone, anyone, to hear me.

"I know what you are thinking," she said, retaking her seat as she wound up her whip. Her eyes remained focused on mine. "You want to scream loud enough for someone to hear, no? I know this not from intuition but from experience. I assure you, no one can hear you. And no one is coming for you. I have been doing this for a long time and know how not to get caught. No one knows where you are, and no one will ever find you."

She paused after her death speech, which would have made me soil my pants if I had been wearing any. I wasn't sure if she wanted to hear my sobbing whimper or if she was thinking, but she just sat there like a statue, staring at me. Her head then tilted to one side, and her eyes focused on the blood gushing from the hole where my nipple used to be. She leaped from her chair toward me, leaned in, and kissed my fresh wound. The kiss was hard and deep, stinging my wound. I screamed in fury as the pain spread through my entire chest. She stood straight and looked me in my eyes. And for the first time, I could see how cold, dark, and void her pupils were. They were just as dark as the darkness from which she emerged. She softly wrapped her hands around the back of my head and asked, "Did you like my dreams?" before kissing her blood-stained mask on my lips. She walked back to her chair to sit in front of me again.

"What do you mean, your dreams? What dreams did you have?" I asked, spitting the blood on the floor.

"Not dreams I have, but dreams I give you."

"I'm confused. What dreams did you have? How can you give me a dream? That's not possible."

"Tell me, do you know how to best attack a man?"

"What?! No. And what does that have to do with my dreams? What did you do to me?"

"Allow me to have my fun, Denzel, or I will create my own." She said, throwing another object at me from under her chair. This time, she didn't miss. The object struck me square in my abdomen, lodging deep in my flesh. I looked down and saw a black-throwing star with silver points. My blood squirted out in small amounts from around the star. I yelled in pain once again.

"You choose," she said calmly.

I knew what she was doing. She was teaching me the only way to avoid torture was to play her little mind game. Hopefully, it would buy me enough time that someone would find me. There aren't many places in the Hampton Roads area where someone won't hear you scream.

"I don't know how to attack any person," I said, panting for air, trying not to breathe too deeply. "I guess surprise attack?"

"No. A surprise attack will only work if the opposition is not a true enemy. If they are a true enemy, then attack is always imminent." She leaned back in her chair, letting one arm dangle over the back. She was brilliant, strategic, sadistic, and enjoying all of this. "The best way to attack a man is through the mind. This is the same method used in American slavery, no? Destroy the mind, destroy the man."

"So, is that what was wrong with me today? You were destroying my mind?"

"An oversimplification, but yes." I couldn't see her mouth but could hear her smile when she knew I was catching on.

"Well, please enlighten me on how you did that. It felt like my brain was being fried from the inside out."

She laughed. "I must thank you. I am very pleased with your observation results."

"You sound like I was your experiment."

"One of many. Every alteration yields different results. Yet, consistency remains key."

"I don't understand," I interjected, silently urging her to keep talking.

"Why not? You will die soon enough." She crossed her legs, leisurely caressing her latex-covered breast. "It is called Dream-Land. A serum of my design. It paralyzes you while inducing hallucinations, but altered to turn even the slightest nightmare into a horrifying reality."

"Dream...Land?" I stuttered, realizing I wasn't going insane. "Well, Simone, your serum works wonders. I mean, I was losing it. I punched a guy at work and nearly lost my job. It's been the worst day of my life. I swear, I learned my lesson. If you would just let me go, I promise to change." As I spoke, she flung another star past my head, a reminder of her lethal capabilities. How many more of those does she have?

"Do not beg. The others begged. Begging is boring, and you are not like others."

"What others?" I asked, feeling her eyes boring into me once again. Why does she stare at me like that? It's like she's a computer, calculating her every move ten times over.

"Why do you think I am here, Denzel?" She rose from her chair, slowly retreating into the darkness until she vanished from sight.

"Uh, if I can be honest and keep my other nipple, I would say that you are hell-bent on killing men. But if that's not the right answer, to teach me a lesson and scare me into being a better man?" I offered a sympathetic grin, hoping to diffuse the tension.

"You are funny. Tell me, did Tara laugh at your jokes?"

My heart sank at the mention of her name. Could this be about her? "Who is Tara?" I nervously stammered.

"You know very well who Tara is. She is the reason I am here. But I want to hear it from you." From the darkness, her whip lashed out, tearing a chunk of flesh from my back.

I let out a pained scream. "Hear what?" I gasped for breath.

"What happened to Tara?"

"I have no idea what happened to her. If she's missing or something, I don't know. I hadn't seen Tara since before she had her miscarriage. Did something happen-"

Before I could finish, a long, shiny steel sword descended down the middle of my chest, sending shivers down my spine. As the sword reached my navel, she rotated it to a carving angle and swiftly sliced through my skin. Agony engulfed my chest as the flap of skin hung separate from my torso, swaying ominously.

"Do not lie to me. I want the truth. Do not be like the others. Be yourself," her voice dripped with annoyance.

I stared at the pool of blood forming beneath me, reflecting on the path that brought me to this gruesome moment. My disregard for love, my malicious intentions, my callous actions—each contributing to this damning culmination. With a heavy heart, I confessed, "I beat the baby out of her. The night she told me she was pregnant. I beat the baby out of her." It was the truth I had long buried, never intending to confront. "I don't know what happened. It was as if I witnessed someone else committing such a horrific act, so unlike me, yet I couldn't intervene. It was like I was a mere spectator in my body." Tears streamed down my cheeks. "I begged her to get an abortion, but she refused. I knew if she had the baby, Gianna would never marry me. The pressure was unbearable, and I snapped. Of all the regrets in my life, that is my greatest. I was consumed by selfishness, blinded to the hearts and lives I shattered. So, perhaps I deserve to die. If you are going to end me, please, let it be swift." Silence hung in the air after my plea for death. Perhaps my raw admission caught her off guard. Maybe she had anticipated my continued facade. I could possibly use this vulnerability to negotiate my freedom.

"I lied to everyone I encountered," I continued, my voice tremulous. "I treated everyone as mere spectators in the performance of my life, presenting the version they desired, not the depressed, suicidal kid yearning for more time with his mother. This is my life's wreckage, one misstep leading to another. The world would be better off without me."

"This is why you are different, my sweet. You possess a good heart, a rarity among men in your situation." I heard her spit on the ground. "Unfortunately, they only realize this when my blade pierces their hearts. They cling to the facade of innocence until it's too late. This pursuit of truth is my pleasure, a rush unlike any other. Holding vile men accountable for the atrocities the world overlooks—it's intoxicating." She stepped back into the light, casting a shadow on the ground. "You are a significant milestone. And to have it come at the hands of a man who beat a child out of a woman... it has become personal. So, you can imagine my disappointment upon discovering the kindness and brokenness within you."

"Does that mean you will let me go?" I implored as she stepped fully into the flickering candlelight, her whip in hand. "Please, I don't want to anger you. I'm begging for my life."

She stood there, head cocked to the side, her intentions veiled behind an unreadable expression. What was she contemplating? Would she spare me or seal my fate?

In a lightning-swift motion, she hurled her whip toward my knee. The crack of impact echoed as my kneecap gave way. I screamed in agony and terror, feeling weak and lightheaded from the pain and blood loss.

"I am here on a mission," she stated, rolling her whip back up. "And I will see it through to the end. I acknowledged your uniqueness, Denzel, but that doesn't grant you immunity." She approached me, her touch sending shivers of revulsion through me as she stroked my hanging penis and cupped my testicles. "I've invested too much in you to simply release you."

Struggling to catch my breath, I managed to ask, "What do you mean, invested?"

She tugged on my testicles, a slow and deliberate force that felt as though she intended to tear them from my body, relishing every moment of my agony. I screamed louder than before, and my hope shattered. I knew I wouldn't leave this place alive.

"Do you think this is easy for me? Do you think I haven't planned, manipulated, and sacrificed my own morals to have you?" She delivered a brutal right hook to my jaw, her knuckles unforgiving. "You naïve American coward! In my country, pain is a birthright. Accept your punishment like a man. Did you stop when Tara begged you to? You nearly killed her." Another blow landed on the opposite side of my jaw, followed by a strike to my forehead and a knee to my stomach, the assault relentless and merciless.

"You will pay with your life for what you've done," she declared, unsheathing her sword. The sound of the blade slicing the air filled me with dread as she pointed it downward. "But you will not suffer needlessly. I will grant you a swift death because of your good heart." With a final, chilling farewell, she aimed the sword at me. I heard a faint kissing sound from beneath her mask.

My entire body felt limp, the weight of it pressing against the rope tethering me in place. I drifted in and out of consciousness, fixated on the sword's tip aimed at me. But it didn't plunge toward my chest; instead, it hung motionless in the air. She hesitated, then abruptly turned and sliced cleanly through the candles, plunging the room into darkness.

"Yo Z! Denzel, you here?!" A distant voice called out, barely audible in the pitch-black room. Unsure if my eyes were open or closed, I refrained from responding. I didn't want to lead any potential rescuer into a trap set by Simone, so I lifted my head skyward and silently prayed for deliverance. The voice grew louder, then faded. As my head swam and a bone-chilling cold enveloped me, my consciousness slipped away, and I saw darkness once again.

When I awoke, the rhythmic beeping of a monitor filled the air. It was a sound I recognized—a vital signs monitor. Fear gripped me. Was I still in a dream? Would Simone still be here if I dared to open my eyes?

Driven by a loud banging sound nearby, I reluctantly opened my eyes, only to be met with blinding light and excruciating pain coursing through my body. My head throbbed as I struggled to adjust to the brightness. A fiery agony flared from my sternum to my navel, where Simone had inflicted her cruel cut.

"Z! I'm here. I'm here. I just ran into the chair. You're safe," Devon's voice reassured me as he leaned over my bed, kissing my forehead. "I thought I lost you, bro."

"What happened? Where am I?" I croaked, my voice hoarse and strained.

"You're at Saint Paul in the ICU."

"Is this a dream? Am I dreaming? Are you real, Devon?"

Devon chuckled. "Damn right, I'm real. Real enough to save your naked ass from getting murdered."

"Naked? Murdered? Simone?" My thoughts tumbled out in confusion. "Where is she?"

"I don't know who it was or where she is. I didn't see anyone when I opened the warehouse door. Just you, bleeding and strapped up. I didn't ask questions. I just got you down to the nearest hospital, and they transferred you here."

"Wait, rewind. Warehouse door? What warehouse?"

"I found you in a warehouse in Suffolk's Industrial Park. Took me forever to find your car."

"How did you even know where to look for me?"

"The watch I gave you." His words jogged my memory, reminding me of the watch I had left in my BMW's armrest.

"I thought you might have forgotten it in the car after I told you never to take it off. Turns out it was a stroke of luck because that's how I found you."

"How did you know something was wrong?"

"After you left our place, I watched your car from the window. I had a bad feeling about everything happening to you. Then, when you drove off, I saw this car park down the block, start its engine, and follow you. At first, I thought it was a coincidence, but when you didn't answer my calls, I knew something was off. I went to your apartment, but you and your car were gone. So, I tracked the watch. Guess this is one time I'm glad you didn't listen to me."

It was all real. I couldn't believe it. Tears streamed down my face as I offered a silent prayer of gratitude for my life. I turned away from Devon, unable to comprehend how close I had come to death. I replayed the flashes of her sword slicing through my chest, the searing pain of her whip tearing at my skin. The sheer horror of it all was overwhelming. My life had been hijacked, manipulated, and nearly extinguished by her. I was nothing more than a pawn in her twisted game—a game where I had become her personal milestone, a target for her sinister ambitions. Now, I was the one who had escaped, the only one who had slipped through her grasp. But with every sign pointing to me knowing too much—about her, about her serum—I realized I had become a threat to her identity, safety, and freedom. And deep down, I knew this was just the beginning.

CHAPTER 16

AN ASSASSIN'S JOURNAL

DreamLand Log Entry #23

Target Name: Denzel Eugene Williams (Nickname' Z')

Bio: Born April 18th, 1982

Residence: Virginia Beach, VA

Mother: Laverne Williams. AKA Verna. Died 1990. Reasons: UNK.

Father: UNK

Occupation: Pediatric Surgeon with St. Joseph's Pediatric Hospital

Crime against humanity: Beating unborn child out of a former lover.

Execution of contract

As usual, my handler presented Denzel's contract to me in an unlabeled manila envelope left in my mailbox. As I read through the file, it stirred memories of the pain and anguish inflicted by my father. This time, it felt personal. I wanted to savor this assignment, but it didn't unfold as I had hoped for various reasons.

It had been two years since my last assignment when I received Denzel's contract. I vividly recalled the exhilaration of my previous job.

**Note to self...review the last contract.*

Denzel's case was unlike any other. My usual targets were money and power-hungry men who believed they were above consequences. They got what they deserved. Yet, I always endeavored not to let my judgments cloud my execution. Making it personal was never the plan. However, with Denzel, I couldn't help myself. He was the epitome of evil to me—a pediatric surgeon capable of ending a child's life in the womb and then carrying on with his practice as if nothing had happened. Only a true sociopath could commit such acts. My father was a sociopath, and Denzel would meet a similar fate. I wasted no time in preparing for his demise.

Digging into Denzel, my first step was to check his social media accounts. They were all active, yet there were no recent status updates or likes—complete social silence. His last post dated back six months, expressing nervousness. Clearly, he had isolated himself for a reason. This meant I'd have to work harder. I hate conducting field scouting blind to the environment. Renting a hotel and car would only draw attention and leave a paper trail. Fortunately, Virginia Beach was only a three or four-hour drive away, making it feasible for weekend trips without using my personal time at work.

On my first weekend excursion, armed with his last known address, I located the house Denzel shared with his would-be wife at the time. Arriving in his neighborhood as the sun set, I found it picturesque and serene. Parking a few blocks away in the parking lot, I began stretching for an unsuspecting jog to his residence. Dressed in jogging shorts and a loose-fitted tank top, I pulled my hat over my face and set off toward Denzel's house. Surprisingly, the neighborhood was quiet and still despite the beautiful spring evening. It worked to my advantage, minimizing my exposure and sparing me from awkward small talk.

I turned onto his street and found his house obstructed by his neighbor's oversized, overcompensated hedge. Darting past the wall of green ivy leaves, I noticed the for-sale sign planted on Denzel's unkempt lawn. The sight infuriated me. This was my only lead. Denzel had vanished, taking everything I needed to know. Frustrated, I circled his block and headed back to my car, deciding to use the time for a workout since this had been a complete waste.

As I jogged, I mulled over my dead end, searching for a way out. Somewhere amid my thoughts, memories of Edward resurfaced. Yes, him again. I couldn't shake him from my mind; a part of him remained etched in my soul. Then, I remembered the USBkill device he had given me to hack my number six. Realization dawned—I could use the same tactic with Denzel and knew exactly where to deploy it. The hospital where he worked had all the information I needed. The only question was: how would I gain access to hack into the database?

Once back in my apartment, slightly frustrated, I took a shower and settled into bed, researching St. Joseph's Pediatric Hospital, focusing on its IT department. The supervisor, Dana Roberts, appeared in my search results—a 46-year-old chubby recent divorcee, if his social media was to be believed. His feed was littered with images of him clubbing with women half his age and lewd posts accompanied by laughing emojis. He seemed to be at the height of a mid-life crisis, and frankly, he disgusted me. But I saw potential in his weakness. Men like him couldn't resist flirtation, especially in the workplace.

Throughout the week, I fine-tuned the formula for the DreamLand serum. Initially, the dreams inflicted on my victims had been exhilarating. However, I had reached a plateau; the dreams were becoming repetitive and dull. Lately, I have been contemplating ways to manipulate the dreams produced by the serum. I wanted to not only induce nightmares but also integrate them into the victims' lives somehow. This would allow me to toy with their minds for extended periods and push the boundaries of my serum further than I had ever imagined. Denzel was the key to making it happen—it all seemed perfectly aligned.

A week before the mission started, I drove back down to Virginia Beach to Saint Joseph's Hospital. Sitting in the parking lot, I downed mini bottles of vodka, psyching myself up to exit the car. I knew the plan, but I detested it. Nevertheless, there was no alternative—I had to see it through. Waiting until I spotted a group heading to the smoke pit, I emerged from my car wearing black leggings and a dark grey hoodie, with only a bra underneath. I felt exposed, but it was the ideal attire for an off-shift night crew custodian, or so I hoped. Approaching the group as they lit their cigarettes, I needed to establish a good rapport to gain access to the building. So, I asked if I could bum one. An older Black man obliged, noticing I was a new face. I spun a tale about just starting and managed to join them on their way into the building. Every second of the conversation during the walk felt insincere; I loathed the fake laughter at their meaningless banter about supervisors and lazy employees. But it worked. I explained I didn't have a badge yet, and Joe, who lent me the cigarette, swiped me in. He winked at me, perhaps assuming he had a chance because we were both Black. I wanted to recoil in disgust, but I had to stay focused. I smiled and excused myself to the nearest bathroom.

Earlier that week, I had called the hospital front desk, pretending to need directions for an interview. The receptionist informed me that the IT department was located on the ground floor at the back of the hospital. I just needed to get there undetected. Placing earbuds in my ears with the jack in hand in my pocket, I strolled to the IT department, head held high but eyes averted. Surprisingly, gaining access to the department was straightforward. It was a little after midnight, and I had anticipated some commotion or people walking around. Instead, everyone seemed ensconced in their cubicles, headphones on, typing away at their keyboards. Making my way to the back of the office, I knocked on Dana's door. Opening it just enough to peek inside, I saw nothing but the light on. Pushing the door open fully, I almost collided with Dana Roberts, who was walking toward the door. Startled, I laughed it off, claiming I had forgotten his trash, and remarked that he looked familiar. His blue eyes perked up, and he stuttered in response—I knew I had him. Fabricating a story about meeting at a club where he promised to buy me a drink but vanished, I played up my disappointment. He apologized, closed the door to his office, and offered me a seat. I accepted and eventually talked my way into performing oral sex on him in his office. It made me feel sick to my stomach, especially when he exposed himself. However, I needed access to his computer at any cost. Removing my sweatshirt, I revealed my bra, pressing my cleavage together for him to admire. I began to perform oral sex on him before having second thoughts. Just as I started, his door flew open, and another person stood there mouth agape. I tried to hide my face as Dana ushered the idiot out of his office and locked the door.

Just my luck that I would have to put him back in my mouth. I pretended to be embarrassed but continued pleasing him, not wanting to lose the moment. When I couldn't take any more of him trying to stick his cock down my throat, I pulled my syringe of tranquilizer strapped to my ankle and stuck the needle in his thigh. A few seconds later, he was out. I grabbed the badge hanging from around his neck and unlocked his computer. I pulled the USBkill device from its case in my jacket pocket and plugged it into the computer.

Once I downloaded everything I found on Denzel—his past, emails, work browser history, everything—I also saw a close acquaintance of his work in the IT department. I clicked on his file and saw that it was the same idiot who walked into the office. That was a potential problem that I had to handle in due time. I transferred his files as well and snuck out of the hospital.

Reviewing all the files on Denzel, I discovered his work for the community and his crusades for starving children. It made me sick to think of his crimes. I looked at pictures of him with so many kids who didn't know what kind of monster he was. It made me think about my father and took me off my game.

My desire to control the dreams made me think of planning tragedies based on my victim's past to have lingering effects, even after they have woken. Denzel lost his mom at a young age and beat the child out of a woman. Denzel's entanglement with childhood trauma is my key to real and pure pain. I planned to cause an accident involving children that would signal genuine pain that would break his soul. This step in my plan was also my failure. I only intended to blow a tire on the school bus. Except I placed the bomb too close to the exhaust line. I was supposed to give the kids a broken arm, at worst, a concussion. I never intended for someone to die. I swore to him I would only hurt those who deserved it, but I got too deep in my rage and lost sight of myself. When I thought of Denzel, I thought of my father and my hate for him. That made me vulnerable and gave me a debt of consequences. At the moment, I was oblivious to the harm I would cause, only thinking about the excitement from the pain I would inflict on Denzel.

Once I had planned everything, I drove down four days before the night of the initial attack. I needed to find my proxy. The proxy

I used on number nine made my job easier and kept me from getting recognized. I rented a hotel under one of my fake identities and logged on to an escort website on my laptop. I scrolled through the list, looking for the perfect proxy, until I found Simone. She was also black but had long, sexy dreadlocks. She looked perfect, so I hired her for a week for the girlfriend experience. When I met her, I sobbed up my history to her. I told her I was here to get payback on my ex and how he beat our unborn child out of me, eventually telling her how I wanted to kill him. After a day of some well-played acting, she was on my side. I wish you could have seen it. She held me while I cried, and then that turned into us kissing and then orgasms.

When I got Simone on board, my plan was in motion. Monitoring Denzel's emails, I knew they were going to the Granby theatre, and I filled Simone in on her part. Her job was to go into the club, attract Denzel, and get him to take her to his apartment, where I was waiting. She couldn't seem easy or desperate. I told her to walk away from him at some point. That'll get him on the hook for the chase.

We got to the Granby Theater before Denzel, and I pointed him out to her at the bar. She walked over, and I played the background close to them. I saw them talk briefly at the bar and then head to the smoke pit towards the back. I followed and walked out shortly after the door closed behind them. I stood in the shadows, pretending to smoke a lit cigarette. I saw her try to walk away, and he grabbed her arm to keep her there. When he turned his back to me, I slipped out behind a group of frat guys coming to smoke.

I knew Simone had him in her palm, and he was completely unaware. While she worked him back to his place, eventually, I was already on my way there. I parked in a visitor's space and sat to take the neighborhood in momentarily. It was a quiet neighborhood, obviously rented to well-established people. It had a small fountain in the middle of the complex and luxury cars in its resident-only spaces. I got out, still in my fitted dress with my duffle bag hanging from my shoulder, and walked to his apartment. The lighting of the complex was well-lit, to my dismay. But it was only a short walk to Denzel's apartment on the first floor. And then, after picking his lock, I was in his living room within seconds.

His apartment was bleak. The living room featured a poorly mounted TV and a cracked brown leather couch. Exercise clothes filled his closet, while takeout boxes and beer occupied his refrigerator. He lived as if he were a 20-year-old or a mid-life divorcee. With some time to spare, I set up my makeshift IV pole with normal saline and my serum, going over my calculations for my advanced DreamLand serum.

About an hour and a half later, I heard something rustling against the front door of his apartment, and I hurried to my position in the hall bathroom. Simone was supposed to meet me there as soon as she got in to receive a tranquilizer-filled syringe. To keep him unsuspecting, I instructed her to undress once she was inside the bathroom. His focus would be so much on her naked body that he wouldn't even notice her hands holding the syringe behind her back.

I waited anxiously for her to return to the bathroom once he was knocked out. I'm always nervous being in the background, waiting. The lack of control is why I didn't want to use proxies when I started. It wasn't until she returned that I could relax and smile. She told me she stuck the needle in his ass just as he entered her, but unfortunately, this left her trapped when the drug kicked in, and he landed on top of her. I tried hard not to laugh as she explained how she had crawled from under him.

I entered the room with an anxious smile, nervous to see if my dream manipulation would work. Retrieving the IV pole I had stashed in his closet with my beautiful translucent blue DreamLand serum, I walked over to the bed, dragging the pole of hanging fluids, and stared at him for a while as he slept. The evil unconscious looked as peaceful as the innocent.

Hooking up the IV and starting the fluids, I watched the slow drip of the liquids before exiting the room to find Simone standing in the living room. I handed her my keys and told her I would meet her at the hotel on Monday to start phase two. Before she left, Simone asked me if I was sure I wanted to do this. She mentioned that he didn't seem like the type of person I had described, sharing that he mentioned battling his demons and mistakes, and all he wanted was to be happy with someone who loved him. I assured her he was a master manipulator and kissed her before she departed.

I woke up beside Denzel Sunday morning, still asleep from the serum. I realized I had forgotten to put a catheter in last night with all my excitement, but luckily, he hadn't urinated in the bed. After I inserted his catheter, I headed out to place the bomb on the bus. During my scout, I located a bus scheduled for a recreational softball team playing in a summer league, with ages ranging from 13 to 16, tough enough to withstand a car wreck from a blown tire. After I placed the bomb and timed the detonation, I returned to Denzel's apartment.

My hypothesis involved whispering in his ear to judge if the dosage was sufficient by assessing his auditory responses. However, what I hadn't anticipated was the waiting. Typically, my victims met their demise swiftly, with my blade piercing their hearts by daybreak and their heads and hands missing soon after. But this was the first time I found myself spending extended time with a victim, which was more humbling than I had expected. Nevertheless, nothing would deter me from my goal.

I retrieved my tape recorder from my bag and recorded myself uttering random keywords based on his life, such as "mother" followed immediately by "death" or "children" followed by "death." And "fire," well, you get the concept. I set the recording on a constant loop, placed the recorder by his ear, and left the room. I ordered food on his credit card and watched TV in his living room. That was pretty much all I did until very early Monday morning. Around 2 am, I removed his IVs and catheter, packed up, and left. Everything I brought was taken, except for the post-it note I left under his pillow, pretending to be from Simone.

After leaving Denzel's, I returned to the hotel, where Simone was asleep on the bed. I climbed in, and we slept together until almost noon. Upon waking up, Simone turned on the TV, which then cut to news coverage of the bomb exploding on the bus. The giddiness I had attempted to conceal turned to shock when I realized the severity of the situation. It had drawn too much attention. We needed to move on to phase 2 and quickly.

I tracked Denzel's phone, which hadn't moved from the hospital until around 6:40 when he drove to his friend Devon's house. That was my window of opportunity to strike. I drove Simone down to Denzel's location and parked where we could sit and watch his car. Later that night, when I saw him walking to his car, I told Simone to follow the plan and climbed into the trunk through the backseat. I heard her start the car and slid around as she pulled off and made a U-turn to follow him.

I felt the car stop and heard a horn honk, then Simone's muffled voice. Simone's message to my burner phone told me he was on the hook. As the car started, I texted her the instructions on how to drug him. She was to put on the lipstick I gave her, which was a sealant for her lips. After a few minutes, it dried, and only then was she to put on the lip gloss that contained micro-crystals of my DreamLand formula. She was to take a sip from the brim of his glass. The liquid would dissolve the shell of the crystal and release the drug into his drink. Then, wiped her mouth immediately before the drug went into her bloodstream. My entire plan would have gone to shit if Simone accidentally drugged herself.

After an hour of contemplating all the possible outcomes of my plans, Simone popped open the trunk. She was frantic and once again had second thoughts about Denzel. After we put him in his car, Simone went on a 10-minute rant about how sweet and genuine he was and how horrible his dream was. She said she made up a sentimental back story of her being an immigrant, and he comforted her still. She started to give me second thoughts, but I couldn't let anything throw me off my mission. I reassured her he was a master manipulator and lied, saying this was the same way he lured me in.

After calming her down, I had her take my car back to the hotel and drove Denzel's car myself. I told her I would see her in the morning, a cunning lie.

I had the perfect place to take Denzel. I found an abandoned warehouse in an Industrial Park in Suffolk. After putting on gloves and a swimmer's cap to protect myself from evidence, I drove to Suffolk. When I got in his car, I did my standard inspection and saw a smartwatch in his armrest. I wanted to take it out but chose against it.

Walking into the warehouse, I set up Denzel's torture rack and attached the pulley system to the metal rack. With that and my candles lit, I dragged Denzel into the warehouse and hung him on the device. The device was a pulley constructed after Edward's design. A four-point rope system held the limbs but gave me con-

trol. After Denzel was in position and bound, I slipped into my latex outfit. It felt so good to be in my suit again. I could feel the power of control surging through me as I rubbed my covered body.

In a vast act of disappointment, torturing Denzel didn't unfold as I expected. Initially, I was excited. I hid my voice with a Russian accent, which was the best one yet, in my opinion. I've found that accent to be the most effective with my victims. I struck with precision and power using my whip, throwing stars and sword. But to my dismay, I didn't experience the euphoric sense of completion I thought I would. Simone appeared to be right in her initial analysis of him. Denzel was broken, and no matter how badly I wanted to hate him, to make him like my father, he wasn't. Denzel was a person torn by his past mistakes and had accepted his fate. He reminded me of myself. What's worse, through it all, I felt empathy and affection for him. Something about him drew me closer, no matter how hard I tried to distance myself. I kissed him, not to toy with him, but because I wanted to. When I kissed his wound, it was out of sympathy, as if somehow that would make it all better. I hesitated in all my strikes because I didn't want to see him in agony. I would have ended him quickly if it weren't for Devon showing up. I knew he would be a problem for my mission, but I never acted.

My apartment phone rang, interrupting my journal entry. It startled me because the only people who knew the number were The Society Evolving Violence to Eradicate Nations, or The S.E.V.E.N, as they refer to themselves. It was like a summer camp for individuals with unique killing methods. Their mission statement was credited with stealth and cruel means. But if they were calling my phone, I knew it wasn't good. They contacted no one unless it was for a contract.

I picked up the phone on its fourth ring, stalling for time.

"Hello?" I almost whispered. My anxiety had taken over again, and my voice grew timid.

"A fucking school bus! You blew up a fucking school bus!" The deepened, modified voice blared through the receiver.

"Why would you possibly think that was me?"

"Do you not think eyes were watching you?"

"You were watching me?! I don't like being toyed with." I put the phone on speaker while I quietly and quickly gathered my weapons.

"No need to gather your things, Alexa. If I wanted you dead, I would have taken you out while you were writing in your journal. The truth is you are a liability."

I stopped in my tracks and searched every corner of my living room for a place I could hide from a camera within my apartment. How long were they watching me? And how did they know my name? Maybe that was my first mistake, underestimating the S.E.V.E.N.

The voice continued. "Worrying about the mission you failed to complete would serve you better. My sources say that Denzel is still alive, so you failed and brought too much attention." His modified voice sounded lighter as if he was happy to see me fail.

"Does this amuse you? I told you I don't like-"

"This is no amusement, Alexa, but a second chance. This contract was personal to me as well, and I need to see it completed."

"You're using the words "me" and "I" a lot. Something tells me that the S.E.V.E.N isn't in your plans."

"I was told you were smart."

"By whom?" I inquired.

"That is unimportant. Plus, why do they get all the fun? They recruited us to kill, but they control who, where, and how."

"That's a lot of rebel talk coming from you. A wise person would see your world coming to a crash around you and stay clear."

"A wise person bets on themselves and takes the consequences that come, whatever may."

"Yeah, I'm still unconvinced, and the last thing I need is more heat. Especially when it sounds like a vendetta."

"Tell me, Alexa Donovan, how is it sitting with you that Denzel got away? It kills you, doesn't it? Or at least it will."

"Is that a threat? A fake voice doesn't protect you."

"No threats, only logical reasoning. How long do you expect Denzel to keep his mouth closed about what you did? He is a loose end that needs to be cut."

"You speak of working together, yet you use a voice modifier. Trust is the foundation of any partnership, and you do not sound very trustworthy."

"Well, I can prove my trust to you."

"Oh, yeah? How is that?"

A knock came loud at my front door, the same knock I heard coming through the phone receiver.

"Don't worry. I won't bite," the voice said on the phone.

I clenched my sword and inched slowly to the door. Looking through the peephole was useless because I only saw darkness. My heart beat fast from the unknown dangers on the other side of the door. I swallowed my fear, then swung the door open in a fury. The person standing in front of me was the last person I expected. I was so shocked that I didn't even feel my sword slip through my fingers and hit the floor. I stood, locked-eyed, and said, "What do we do now?"

The End of Book 1.

www.ingramcontent.com/pod-product-compliance
Lightning Source LLC
La Vergne TN
LVHW041250110826
845146LV00005BA/1328

* 9 7 9 8 9 9 0 5 0 3 5 3 3 *